CHRISTMAS TREES AND MONKEYS

CHRISTMAS TREES AND MONKEYS

Collected Horror Stories, Volume 1

Daniel G. Keohane

Bob & Jenny,
Watch those christmas lights!

Writers Club Press
New York Lincoln Shanghai

Christmas Trees and Monkeys
Collected Horror Stories, Volume 1

All Rights Reserved © 2002 by Daniel G. Keohane

No part of this book may be reproduced or transmitted in any form or by any means, graphic, electronic, or mechanical, including photocopying, recording, taping, or by any information storage retrieval system, without the written permission of the publisher.

Writers Club Press
an imprint of iUniverse, Inc.

For information address:
iUniverse, Inc.
2021 Pine Lake Road, Suite 100
Lincoln, NE 68512
www.iuniverse.com

The stories contained herein, including names, characters and places, are works of fiction. Any resemblance to actual persons, living or dead, is entirely coincidental.

ISBN: 0-595-25664-3

Printed in the United States of America

For Janet, my wife and best friend. For your love and support, and the writing coupons, and your cooking, and….

Also, a special dedication to Anne Murphy. You're so much stronger than you realize.

Contents

Chronology	xi
Introduction	xiii
Incineration	3
AM	17
The Monkey on the Towers	27
Feed the Birds	43
The Doll Wagon	51
Redemption	65
Ptolemy	81
Y2 Kay	95
Ritual	107
White Wave of Mercy	117
Bark	133
Lavish	151
The Storm of Generations	173
Two Fish to Feed the Masses	185
Tanner's Bomb	201
About the Author	217

Acknowledgements

There have been many people along this strange and twisted path I'd like to thank, but they're probably charging me per page on this, so I'll have to stick to the highlights.

I thank God for allowing me this life and the people who have given me so much love and support over the years, allowing me to do this writing thing in the first place.

Joe and Marilyn Keohane, Dad and Mom extraordinaire, who gave me life, then saved it on more than one occasion. For their unconditional love and acceptance of their brooding scribe of a son.

Janet, for everything I've mentioned in the dedication, for keeping me honest, your eager critiques of these stories when they arrived fresh from the oven and a thousand more things I couldn't begin to list.

Fran B. Bellerive, for your red (and blue and purple and...) pen. Its markings have made all the difference over the years in how these stories have come out. Thank you, thank you.

For all those who have taken their turns at the critical wheel for one or more of the stories herein, including Mark Lowell, Paul Tremblay and Stephen Dorato (I'm sure I've missed someone and if so I apologize).

Editors June Hubbard, Terry West, Seth Lindberg, S. Kay Elmore, Janice Kirkwood, Tracy Martin, Ed McFadden, Diana Sharples, James

Rasmussen, Suzanne Donahue, Stefano Donati, Mario Kivistik, Brian Keene, Brian A. Hopkins and John Amen, for saying "yes".

To my family, friends and every reader who has taken the time to read my stuff and perhaps enjoyed a little of it. A writer's work is a solitary endeavor, and we spend way too much time in our own heads. Once the story's done, however, it belongs to you. I pray I never lose sight of that.

Chronology

"Incineration" © 1999, originally appeared in the *Cemetery Sonata*

"AM" © 1999, originally appeared in *Bonetree*, later reprinted in *Cemetery Sonata II*

"The Monkey on the Towers" © 1999, originally appeared in *The Orphic Chronicle*

"The Doll Wagon" © 2001, originally appeared in *Poddities: A Creative Tribute to Jack Finney's The Body Snatchers*

"Ptolemy" © 2000, originally appeared in *Electric Wine*

"Y2 Kay" © 1999, originally appeared in *Gothic.Net*

"White Wave of Mercy" © 2002, originally appeared in the *Extremes 4: Darkest Africa*

"Lavish" © 2000, originally appeared in *Fantastic Stories of the Imagination*

"The Storm of Generations" © 2001, originally appeared in *The Pedestal Magazine*

"Tanner's Bomb" © 1999, originally appeared in *Gothic.Net*

"Ritual", "Redemption", "Bark", "Feed the Birds" and "Two Fish to Feed the Masses", © 2002, are making their debut in this collection.

Be gentle with them, they're young…OK, maybe "Redemption" is getting on in years, but I'll save that for the story's introduction….

Introduction

I'd like to take a moment to thank you for picking up and spending your hard-earned dollars for this, my first collection of short stories. Most of what you'll soon read have been published over the past few years in a wide range of publications, from magazines to webzines to anthologies. A few are new, seeing print for the first time. I hope that while you're here you enjoy yourself.

Before each story I take a moment to explain how I came up with the idea, and offer a fact or two that I think you might find interesting. Maybe a fact or two you could have done without. The phrase "Too much information, Dan" is common in my life. I tried to make them enjoyable, and offer a quick insight into the process I sometimes go through in creating these short stories. There are no spoilers in the introductions, I promise—read them before diving into each story and don't worry that I might give away the ending.

Enough of this bantering about. Have a good time, and let me know what you think. I'd love to hear from you. And again, thanks.

Dan

About "Incineration"

It seems fitting that I open the collection with my first published story. After a few years getting my fingers wet with fiction-writing, I stopped. Three children, two jobs and a new house later, I returned to the keyboard. After writing a few new stories, I decided to look back through my old notebook to see if there were any gems left unrealized from before my hiatus. There, I found the opening (two or three paragraphs, hand-written), of a story called "Incineration." These were the last three paragraphs of fiction I'd written before hanging up the smoking jacket and pipe for a time. I never forgot the story. It resurfaced in my frenzied brain at odd times, only to be mentally filed away for another day.

Newly inspired, I wrote the story out beginning to end. Not much changed from what was in my head all those years. Around that time I'd joined a professional organization for writers called the Horror Writers Association. In the HWA's first newsletter, I discovered a plethora of market listings specializing in horror. Magazines and anthologies which never saw even a one-liner in tomes like Writer's Market. One of these markets was an anthology called *Cemetery Sonata*, edited by June Hubbard.

Well, this story takes place in a crematorium, so I thought, why not? I sent it off via email and waited. A couple of month's later Ms Hubbard, God bless her, said she'd buy it. So I soon had thirty-six dollars in my pocket and my very first fiction sale.

Now, they *say* women forget a lot of the physical pain experienced in child birth. If they didn't, they'd stop having children after the first, and our planet would be under populated and primed for invasion by alien races who are just too damned intimidated to attack because there's so many of us hanging around. That's what they say, anyway. Similarly, writers forget all of their dozens (or hundreds) of rejections with that one acceptance. If we didn't, we'd stop writing, and Mr. And Mrs. John Q America would miss out on a lot of creepy stuff, like the following story....

Incineration

The top half of the casket's lid stood open. Patrick, in his quiet terror, began to calculate how he would maneuver himself beside Mister Benchman's body without touching it. A new wave of nausea rolled over him.

Patrick, Kenny and Kenny's best friend Jacob crouched in the grass. The rectangle of yellow light from the basement window was like a camp fire between them. Above the boys, the remnants of the summer day burned away into evening. A thick humid blackness fell around them. They watched the old man approach the coffin, close the lid and twist the ornate brass latch.

Jacob whispered. "Don't worry. You can still get in. The latch won't lock. Just turn it and lift."

Patrick swallowed, wondering again what he was trying to prove. That the son of the town's Baptist preacher wasn't just another wimpy Jesus-lover? That a wimpy Jesus-lover can die as easily as anyone? His father would kill him if he found out. Beat his devil-possessed son to death with one of those massive bibles he preached from. Not for the first time, Patrick decided to get up and leave. Tell Jacob and Kenny to find someone else to jerk around with this stupid dare.

Someone with more guts. He sighed quietly and waited.

The old man stood by the large oven doors, tinkering with a faucet then various switches. He looked to Patrick like a mad scientist from an old black and white movie.

Jacob was moving way too much. He said, "OK. Get ready, Bible Boy."

"Don't call me that."

"Once he fires this sucker up, he'll leave the room while it gets cranking. I've seen it a hundred times. He'll be gone for five minutes. Maybe more."

The old man flipped a switch. The darkness beyond the doors exploded in a brilliant flash of light. Patrick closed his eyes. A minute later Jacob slapped him on the back. "OK, he's out. Let's go."

The casket was closed. Behind the windows in the furnace doors, fire danced like a thousand burning fingers. Kenny, who had said nothing since they left on their bikes from Jacob's house, moved his heavy frame into the square of light. He slid a piece of aluminum along the edge of the window. Something clicked. He lifted the sash and propped it open with the jimmy.

Patrick looked at Jacob. "You never did this."

Jacob glared back at him. "Damn right, I have. Twice. Don't chicken out on me now, or everyone's gonna hear about it."

"I'm not chickening out. I just don't think you ever did it." Laying face-down on the grass, Patrick shimmied backwards. His legs dangled over nothing for a moment, then his toes touched the concrete floor. The faces of Jacob and Kenny hung ghostlike in the window. Darkness beyond them. Patrick let go of the sill.

The room smelled like the science lab at school. Chemicals, Bunsen burners. Looking around, there wasn't much to see besides a desk, four folding chairs, and the coffin. He'd better get this over with before the old man came back and pushed it into the oven with him inside. Patrick thought of being trapped, burned alive with the corpse of Mister Benchman. He walked toward the coffin.

The latch turned easily. Patrick lifted the upper lid. The head of Mister Benchman did not turn towards him with an evil grimace, as he'd half-expected. The sunken face was covered in too much makeup. The storekeeper didn't look right. Where was the smile? Whenever Patrick and his father came into Selver's Variety the man always had a smile.

The platform was metal mesh wrapped around rollers. He gave the coffin a shove to make sure it wouldn't roll against the furnace doors. It didn't. It sat low to the floor. Patrick had no problem climbing up alongside. He remembered the last time he saw this man alive. When his father had gone back to the cooler for a forgotten jug of milk, Mister Benchman handed Patrick a Three Musketeers candy bar. The boy immediately had shoved the treat deep into his windbreaker's pocket, prayed his father hadn't seen it. Candy was forbidden in their world; both Patrick and Mister Benchman knew that. The storekeeper simply smiled as usual, never letting on to this dark new secret as the preacher returned with the milk. That was one month ago, and Patrick only garnered enough courage to eat the damned Three Musketeers three days ago. That was the day he heard Mister Benchman was dead.

He worked his left leg into the coffin, wincing in reaction to the stiff, papery feel of the man's leg. There was no way he'd get in there without touching the guy.

"Hurry up, you idiot." Jacob's head poked into the room. "He'll be back in three minutes." Patrick wondered how Jacob was keeping such precise time, since none of them wore a watch.

"You just make sure you throw the pebble when a minute's up."

"Two minutes."

"One minute. I'm not getting caught by that old guy."

"Whatever! Just do it."

Patrick sat on the edge and put his other foot inside the coffin. He looked up.

"Show me the pebble."

Jacob was about to say something, thought better of it, then reached into his pants' pocket. He held the pebble between two fingers. Patrick turned away from the window, trying not to look disappointed.

The coffin was uncomfortable. Under the frills and satin sheet was nothing more than the wooden bottom. No cushions, no soft down bedding. Patrick pushed his way over the curls of the sheets. His eyes blinked away sweat.

"Close the lid." From the window, Jacob's voice sounded breathy, like he'd been running. "Close it. Close it."

Patrick slowly reached over the dead man and grabbed the inside of the lid. The move brought his face too close to Mister Benchman. Vomit wormed its way into the boy's throat. He closed the lid as fast as he could, turned his head away and threw up. It splattered across his shoulder. The acidic smell filled the cramped interior, intensified by the increasing heat of the oven. In the coffin's complete blackness, facing away from the wooden figure beside him, Patrick felt an urge to cry.

Instead, he counted. One. Two. Three. His tongue tasted sour, as if he'd drunk a glass of bad milk. This mental image sent more vomit against the coffin's wall. Patrick spit out a chunk of something caught in his cheek. *Don't think about anything*, he thought. *Just wait for the pebble.*

The sound of the basement door opening was muffled from inside his tomb, but Patrick knew instantly that he had lost. The old man was back.

* * * *

Moments earlier, Jacob watched Patrick lean over the dead man and close the lid. He tried to swallow, but his mouth couldn't work up any spit. Once the coffin was closed, Jacob shifted his position until he lay belly-down on the grass. He had to. The erection in his jeans made crouching too uncomfortable. Since a few months after his twelfth birthday, this had become a new twist in his life. This time, it was not received with the terror and embarrassment he'd suffer in the middle of Miss Monroe's Social Studies class. This time it felt right. Jacob's stomach tightened at the thought of Patrick laying alone with the corpse, and the fact that he had no intention of tossing the pebble. He stared at the flames licking each other behind the furnace windows. His arousal intensified.

"Come on, man," Kenny said, leaning back on his haunches. "This is just too sick. Throw the rock so we can get the hell out of here."

For as long as the two boys were old enough to cross the street, they had been each other's only friend. This may have been because they were the only kids their age on that end of Washington Street. More likely it was because their mutual obsession with all things macabre alienated them from the rest of their classmates. Last Thursday, Kenny brought Patrick into their fold. Now, he couldn't help thinking that Jacob concocted this scheme just to scare away the threat Patrick presented to their long-standing twosome.

Jacob continued his vigil and waved away his friend's suggestion. Kenny grabbed his arm. "Throw it, you piss-head."

At that moment the door to the small room swung open.

In a reaction more instinctive than calculated, Jacob slapped at the metal bar. He caught the window at the last moment, closing it silently. His eyes never left the old man. Carefully, like an animal backing away from a threat, he slithered in the grass until he was out of the window's light.

Kenny whispered, "Oh, my God." He was on his feet, pacing behind Jacob. "Oh, my God oh my God oh my—"

"Will you shut up?" Jacob's hiss froze Kenny's hysteria for the moment. The boy looked down, eyebrows raised in a silent plea.

In reply Jacob whispered, "We do nothing." He scrambled onto his knees. "Just stay put and see if he leaves again."

Kenny shook his head, but did not move.

* * * *

Benson Laraby shuffled past the coffin. In his peripheral vision he tried to see if the Kinsley boy was still at the window. He had seen someone up there earlier. He knew damned well who it was. *Sick idiot kid*, he thought. This was the third time he'd spied the boy watching him. He turned to face the window. Nothing but darkness beyond. He sighed. The boy was probably still there but, as before, the old man decided to leave him to his devices rather than call Robert Kinsley and get him in trouble. Last thing he wanted was a bunch of broken windows to deal with later.

The internal temperature looked good. Laraby released the safety and pulled down hard on the old lever. The twin doors to the oven screeched open. In seconds the basement room was thick with heat.

* * * *

Patrick took short, silent breaths. He listened to the old man's footsteps. All but forgotten was the stench and feel of the vomit. Two opposing voices in his head fought for control. One screamed "Open the lid! Open it and climb out the window. He'll see you but might not recognize you! You'll be safe...."

The other voice was calm, a soothing unperturbed whisper. "Don't move," it said. "Just stay calm and wait to see what happens. The last thing you want is for Jacob to see you running like a little girl. The old man'll recognize you; don't kid yourself. Then what will your father say?"

This last voice is what Patrick obeyed.

Something shifted beside him. He turned his head in the darkness. With terrifying clarity he realized the only other thing in the coffin was Mister Benchman.

* * * *

When Kenny pushed past his friend, Jacob grabbed him by the shoulders and pulled him down. In the boy's ear he whispered, "What do you think you're doing?"

"The old man's gonna burn him, we have—"

Jacob covered Kenny's mouth with his hand. "You're right," he said, looking occasionally through the window. "Little Patrick's going to burn. The doors are open. The old man's going to pull another lever and the coffin'll slide in and the doors will slam shut." He smiled and wiped at a string of spit with his free hand. "There's nothing we can do now but watch him die."

Kenny shifted sideways, sending Jacob rolling in front of the window. "You're nuts, man. I'm not letting him die!"

Jacob saw the old man move to put the casket between him and the furnace. The burning in his belly was now an inferno. Kenny crawled towards the window. Jacob jumped on top of him. Kenny dragged himself along the ground. He was seconds away from ruining everything. With both hands Jacob lifted the biggest rock within reach and crashed it onto the back of the other boy's head. Kenny grunted only once. His left arm twitched, as if trying to shake off a bug, then stopped. He lay, unmoving, just outside the square of yellow light.

Something dark turned in Jacob's stomach. He ignored it, knowing that Kenny would start bawling at any moment. He looked through the window and hoped he hadn't missed anything. He watched with renewed excitement as the old man pulled the final release, sending the casket rolling along the conveyor and into the oven.

* * * *

For one joyous moment Patrick thought the old man was gone. The footsteps faded behind his head, towards the door. Was he gone? The oven doors must have been opened. The roaring of the furnace muffled most of the outside sounds. He wished he could be sure.

The calm voice returned. "Stay where you are. Don't blow it now."

"Patrick, run!" The other voice, still heard only within his head, sounded different, not his own. It sounded like Mister Benchman. Still half-turned in the darkness towards the body, Patrick pushed himself against the vomit-covered wall. He heard the sound again, the rustling of polyester, cloth rubbing against itself. The coffin shook. Patrick had the sensation of riding on a roller coaster.

The howl of the furnace raced around him. The old man hadn't left. He just rolled them in. Suddenly, it seemed too late to do anything. If he opened the lid, he'd be burned alive. Patrick's mind spun in a chaotic jumble of thoughts. If he didn't do something now he'd burn anyway. What would his father say? He closed his eyes, panicked sobs fighting for release. "Don't make a sound," the calm voice said. "Shhhh."

The unmistakable screech of the closing doors. Now he was going to die. Again the sound of rustling beside him. Something grabbed his leg. An arm fell across his chest. Patrick opened his eyes, expecting to see the old man pulling him out. All he saw was darkness. Fingers closed tighter around his leg. Patrick screamed as he'd never screamed before.

*   *   *   *

The oven doors slammed shut. Immediately the shape of the coffin was lost beyond the windows, wrapped in a savage blanket of fire as the gas jets opened completely. Laraby maintained his grip the release lever. That was a scream he heard; it had to be. There was no longer any sound but the roar of the furnace. He looked around, up to the window. At that moment three thoughts crystallized in his mind: he *had* heard someone, the Kinsley kid was at the window earlier, and now he was gone. The old man looked at the oven door, back at the window.

"Oh, shit."

*   *   *   *

"Burn," Jacob breathed. "Burn." He saw the vague outline of the coffin in the flames. "Are you screaming?" He almost laughed the words. He rubbed his hands against the front of his jeans. A sudden, shaking release filled every corner of his body. He sighed in ecstasy. A blinding flash of light forced his hand to his eyes. The doors had been opened. Safety valves kicked in, shutting down the oven.

Jacob leaned into the square of light. He shouted, "No! What are you doing?" The old man pulled the burning husk of coffin through the doors with a grappling hook.

*   *   *   *

Laraby thought he heard shouts behind him, but knew they had to be from inside. The top of the coffin was engulfed completely in flame. The layers of polish had melted, leaving the wood along the sides to blacken and pop. Once the majority of the box was free of the doors the old man grabbed the burning lid. The pain in his hands was instant and immense. He let go and grabbed once more for the grappling hook. His palms sizzled against its handle. He allowed himself a short high-pitched scream. Then he noticed the coffin's latch was open. Why the hell hadn't he seen that before? Above him, fire and smoke licked at the cement roof. The sprinklers did not react, but the fire alarms screamed in panic.

"Come on, oh God this is insane." The coffin just kept burning. Heart smashing in his chest, he maneuvered the hook under the edge of the lid and pulled. The melted hinges fought him every inch. Laraby howled with the effort and the constant pain. The burning lid raised completely.

What he saw in the coffin made him stop. Benchman's body lay sprawled atop a young boy. It wasn't Kinsley. The fire spread to the coffin's lining. Cursing, he flung the dead man away. An arm landed in the fire; the dark jacket's sleeve glowed with red burning spots then ignited.

The kid was heavy, dead weight. Laraby worked his arms under the shoulders and pulled. The side of the coffin was as hot as coals, searing his knees. The boy's legs caught on the lower lid. Laraby slipped and fell onto the floor. He clambered back to his feet, reached into the burning coffin and gripped the boy by the shirt. Beside him, the corpse itself was lighting up. Chemicals pumped through veins to replace blood now burned like gasoline. Laraby pulled the boy from the coffin head first. Together they crashed to the floor.

Black smoke filled the room halfway to the floor. Laraby leaned closer to the boy, but heard no breathing. His fingers were too blistered to look for a pulse. He opened Patrick's mouth and exhaled into it. Once, it seemed, was enough. The boy gasped in the burning air, then coughed with such violence his body twisted on the floor like an epileptic's.

The old man crawled to the door and opened it, hand disappearing into the smoke when he reached for the knob. He pulled the twisting body of the boy out of the room.

* * * *

Smoke drifted under the window; black clouds obscured everything beyond. Jacob wobbled side to side, searching for a break through which to see what was happening. Useless. He found the metal bar; held his breath and propped open the window. Smoke poured into his face. He flattened himself against the ground, coughing once out of reflex. As soon as the cloud beyond the window was spent enough, he raised his head and looked inside.

The wood of the coffin was a blackened, burning log. Within, the crackling bones of Mister Benchman separated from each other as the final licks of flame disintegrated tendons and muscle. Freed of restraint, the skull turned sideways. Jacob stared into two pillars of smoke drifting from the eye sockets. He gripped the tall, neglected grass below the window in an attempt to control his fear. "Where is he?" he whispered. "What did you do with him?" As if to answer, the skeleton's jaw dropped open in a flaming mockery of laughter.

Jacob scurried backwards without taking his eyes from the window. "Come on, Kenny. Let's get the hell out of here."

The other boy did not respond. He lay face down, the rock still resting against his head.

"Kenny?"

A few minutes later, the first fire truck screamed into the yard. In the hellish red glow of the emergency lights, Jacob knelt beside his friend and howled into the night.

About "AM"

There are generally two types of stories I tend to write. *Slam! Bang! Aaaaaahhh!* Meat and Potatoes kind of horror, like the previous story. Then there are the ones I write at night on my one-hundred dollar, text-editor-only laptop, before dropping off to sleep. I do this in lieu of reading when I feel the muse tugging at me. I'll boot up the little PC and sit in bed, type away, then eventually fall asleep mid-sentence. I wake up in the wee hours of the morning, save the file, and turn off the PC. The next night, it usually takes a little while to figure out what the last couple of sentences are supposed to say. You see, I usually fall asleep first, *then* stop typing a few minutes later (sleep-writing, if you will). So the last couple of lines might read:

> The cat bowed its head in an angry fghen sjt. Bentille laughed attt the little shit wha ths she ejejejeje,,,,,,,,,,,,,,,,,,,,,,,,

Many a brilliant writing was lost in the inability of my brain to unscramble lose last lines.

The other off-shoot of these stories is that their atmosphere tends to be more moody and introspective. I become bolder in my approach, experimenting with stuff that sometimes works, sometimes doesn't. In the case of Benedictine in the next story, even his name was a bizarre step. What the hell kind of name is *Benedictine*? It's not a name, but it's perfect for this story…I think. My tired brain probably picked it because of the monk-connection (i.e. Benedictine Monks). Reverence.

Quiet. The story itself came to being on the ride home one night after working late. I was bored of the FM stations, didn't have my usual book-on-tape, so I tried some talk shows on AM. Driving along a deserted Interstate 190, I noticed how so many faraway stations served as background noise, hissing in and out depending on where your car happened to be at the moment.

Hmm, thought I, *maybe these aren't other radio stations, maybe they're*…well, read on.

Oh, I should point out, the bits in the story where I portray radio static was *not* me falling asleep while writing, honest.

AM

Benedictine barely breathed. Just enough to keep himself alive. Otherwise the tenuous line, the milky thread connecting him to the old couple might forever blow away, a breath severing a spider's thread. His fingers did not touch the dial. They merely offered the suggestion of touch, of turning barely a whisper to the left. It shouldn't be able to go this far. There was nothing here to get.

Or so everyone thought. Benedictine knew better. Not to breathe. Just enough. Not to touch.

"…spell it ou…zzzzhssss…me." Static washed over the words, an undertow perpetually pulling the voices back into its depths. "Maybe I'm too sen…zzzzsssshhh…sten properly."

Listen. Savor the clarity for as long as it remains.

Her: "You just never cease to dig your cla…ssskkksszzzindss…my skull. Are you ever happy?"

Him: "Must be th…sssss. Senile me. Fine. Tell me. What the hell did I do this time?"

Oh, God. So clear now. Benedictine looked up, but only with his eyes. A turn of the head might sever the signal. A.M. radio could be a hypersensitive harpy when she chose to. More so this far back on the dial, and such an eternal distance between Benedictine and the bickering couple.

The night sky was clear, crystallized into a billion stars. Odd, since A.M. broadcasts usually traveled better with clouds to reflect from. His eyes returned to the portable radio. He supposed weather didn't really play a factor in this case.

The old woman finally replied. "It's what you didn't do. It's ALWAYS what you didn't s...sssszzzzthh...."

Not so soon! Static. Passing under some celestial overpass? So inconsistent, the signal. He waited.

Benedictine was seventeen years old. He liked this old couple. They argued. Never seemed to give it a rest. This was the third time he'd tuned them in with any semblance of clarity. The first two transmissions were no different than tonight's. Argue. Bicker. Unrelenting, spiteful words, and something else. Did true love mean fighting over eternity? It couldn't be that. Subtle inconsistencies in their voices. Overtones of genuine humor in their rhetoric. Maybe they took some macabre pleasure in each other's biting exchange.

"...zzthlssss..." Silence.

The hissing faded, returned, fell in submission to the signal once again. He hadn't moved the dial. There hadn't even been a breeze. Good fortune.

But silence.

The bickering old man and his nagging wife, both suddenly mute. But the signal was clear, the hissing most definitely fallen under its strength. The two were no longer talking. Benedictine stared at the dial. The grass chilled him, as if every dark blade had begun to grow, digging through the jacket and into his belly, injecting early morning dew like ice.

Silence.

Did they know he was listening? That was stupid. Paranoid. They couldn't hear him, or know he was here. Benedictine looked around the dark landscape. Trees loomed like monstrous pedestrians hovering around an accident, seeming to lean in for a closer look at the man sprawled on his belly in the dark. The man who stared in turn at the portable radio leaning against the granite slab.

Benedictine was alone. Above him, stars ignited more brightly than he could remember. Nothing for miles to compete with their brilliance. No one knew he was here. No one knew he was listening.

But if he could hear them, then why couldn't—

"Well," said the old man, as if tiring of the stalemate. "Like I was saying, maybe you think I should get my head examined." His voice was clear, but somehow devoid of its earlier passion. Speaking as if bored of this play acting. But so clearly, as if uttered from only a few feet away. Benedictine stared at the ground where he lay. "But do you remember when we were in our thirties…I think it was—"

"You were forty-two and I was thirty-nine."

Benedictine jumped at the old woman's voice. Still coming from the tiny speaker, but never before this clear, this loud. As if drifting closer to the surface, bordering their world and his. He didn't like this image invading his thoughts. He rose to his knees, eyes scanning the ground below him. The man rebuked his wife's interruption. "You don't even know what I'm going to say, yet."

"Yes I do…ssszzthh…" The signal fell below the watery white surface of static, a million living souls pushing those lost back under the waves. Benedictine stood holding the radio in one hand. It hissed as if angry, too far from the ground, from the couple. He stared at the twin granite monuments.

They died together, recently, probably arguing all the way to the end. It was a car accident. He'd looked it up at the library. Only eleven months ago. Maybe that was why their signal was so strong. The thought seemed ludicrous.

He walked further back, the shadows of the spectator trees closing in behind him, waiting for his next intrusion. The flashlight's beam bounced across various epitaphs. Some more interesting than others', but still too recent. Here. Twenty years ago. She died three years before he'd been born. Young. Mid-twenties.

As before, Benedictine lay on his belly, turned the dial without turning, barely a hair change in frequency. The needle strained against the furthermost reaches of its man-made restraint, backed against the wall from so many living voices vying for attention.

"sssssssstthhhzzzzzzssssss...sszz..."

There. Something. He leaned forward, hoping the act wouldn't shatter the thin filament drawn out before him.

Silence. No, something. A sob? Clearer now. Someone crying. A voice not from any physical source but audible nonetheless, never faded with time. Not a recent bout of tears, either. A cry grown refined over the years, moving in its own rhythm.

Had she sounded this hoarse in life, he wondered? She uttered a despondent wail for a moment, then slid back into that deeper, heart-splitting sob. Benedictine lay still and listened, staring at the small radio's face as if waiting for an image of the bereft to appear like a genie, if only he watched long enough. Eventually he closed his eyes, rested his head and slept, lulled by the incessant mournful broadcast.

He awoke with a jolt. Benedictine felt heavy as if the river of blood in his veins had frozen while he slept, only now beginning to thaw. How long had he slept? He squinted at the glowing face of his watch. Four twenty-one. Just over two hours. Such a long time to lay outside like this. No sign of a growing dawn in the eastern sky, but it was just a matter of time. Here and there among the trees a morning bird repeated it's lifelong song to the impending light.

Benedictine leaned towards the radio. She continued sobbing. The signal had faded, however, become atrophied. As if the energy used for this broadcast was being slowly spent, used up like the batteries he'd bought for the radio only yesterday. Or perhaps she'd wandered too far in the metaphysical, barren room which entombed her, away from that impossible microphone which perpetually transmitted her cries to the boy laying above her.

He listened. Sorrow. Eternal sorrow at some stricken cause which could never be rendered better. Was she mourning herself, he wondered. Those left living? Maybe the sharp blades of hell allowed her this one respite, enough to let her fall into grieving self-pity, never truly appreciating the reprieve.

Maybe she knew something he didn't, but could do no more than sob her warning through decayed and withered lips.

"Stop this," he whispered.

The crying stopped.

No static raced in to fill the void. After a moment a dry sniffle, then a soft moaning and the deep, deep wailing began again.

Benedictine's heart seemed to pause as she paused. He thought perhaps to repeat his words, experiment, see if they had the same effect. But he didn't dare, didn't want to know.

Standing, he let the sands of worldly interference pour over the spot where he once lay. Then he walked. Static dipped almost imperceptibly past each tombstone. Not enough for anyone not specifically listening for it to notice. And not all the stones caused the effect, either. Sometimes he wondered if perhaps six feet under these particular spots lay an empty coffin. He imagined a vampire long risen, or an embezzler sitting on a beach far from the box in which he never lay, letting it rot and corrode over the years and decades without him.

Back. Further than Benedictine ever dared wander in such complete darkness. He'd come to these graves in daylight, wondering whether he'd have the nerve to listen to their voices when he returned. The trees crowded thickly here, more crooked and expansive in this old section of the cemetery. They swept away the stars, and with them the only source of illumination. Benedictine's flashlight still lay at his previous stop, left to console the weeping young girl with its mechanical objectivity. He stepped carefully, navigating around gray shapes as they emerged like shattered ice flows around him.

Further back still, where the worn and forgotten dates could barely be discerned even in daylight. In the dark the numbers didn't exist. But he knew what they read. "b. 1789—d. 1842." "b. 1702—d. 1767." "b. 1698—d. 1745." That was the one.

The orange flag which he'd placed directly behind the tombstone that morning fluttered in the breeze, sucking any stray light into its colorless florescence. Benedictine pulled the pole from the ground and tossed it away, not wanting its presence to pull his thoughts out of 1745 and into the growing damp light of the present. He lay down with the radio.

The ground felt warmer here. The overhanging trees caught the dew before it landed, pulling it away from this dry, arid spot. Benedictine tried not to move the dial.

"Sssssss....."

The static never quite faded. He rested two fingers on the knob, urging it further back. The plastic needle bent in protest. No further, it said. But a millimeter, a fraction of a millimeter. The static faded. An auditory clue. A sound like paper, wind blowing though a shredded wasp nest, its pieces falling like ash. Benedictine saw these images in his mind, drawn by the sound which rose just beyond the static. A breath? No, it couldn't be. Not a real breath. But something, an exhalation in time.

So old. 1745. Was that a sigh? Perhaps his unwitting host made these sounds more infrequently than the others, time washing away the soul's addiction to such mundane earthly habits.

Benedictine leaned closer to the speaker. The dry grass crackled in his ear.

The voice he heard, the sound it made, made him think of something he'd read a long time ago. How mummies would make this sound when palms were pressed against their corpses to force stale air from the lungs.

"Aaaaahhhh...," the voice said. Then nothing. Silence. Benedictine waited. "...aahhhhh," breathed the wasp nest voice again. Then in a whisper that was more breath than words, "Leave us alone."

He involuntarily shuffled away from the radio. The words had been directed at him. They had to be. They weren't. He was being paranoid again. Slowly, he moved back into his earlier position. But the thought wouldn't go completely away. Had these been the first words uttered from this spot in a hundred years? Two hundred?

"Go home.... leave aaaahhss alone." The man buried two and a half centuries ago took in a slow, paper breath.

"Killing usssss..."

The words drifted around the living boy, no more a part of their originator than the air the dead man continued to exhume. Yet directed. At him. Talking to the trespasser laying atop the grave so long undisturbed.

Benedictine stared at the gray monument in front of him, perfectly smooth in the night, darkened and chipped along the edges in daylight. It marked the spot where a man's body was interred under centuries-old tears. Now the speaker breathed its contempt at what he was doing. Hating him for his wet, beating life. Loathing him for his vision.

"Killing me...." the wind itself seemed to say. It was too much.

Benedictine stumbled to his feet and ran, leaving the radio to lay against the granite marker. An unheard cry from the speaker, an ethereal transmission no longer attended to by the retreating teenager. "...stop...," said the dry, ancient soul, as it slowly leeched from the radio to lift and dissipate like fog in the cool morning air.

About "The Monkey on the Towers"

Yep, we come to the "Monkey" story alluded to in the title of this collection.

The origins of this story go back well before I started seriously writing fiction. Sixteen years earlier, to be exact. I'm stuck in the tailgate of a friend's old station wagon as a group of us head to New Hampshire for a skiing trip. There I was, wedged between sleeping bags and pillows and effectively barred from any conversation. All I could do for the two-and-a-half hour drive was stare out the window. Stare, stare, and let my mind, my imagination, wander, wander, up Route 3, looking out the window, watching the mile markers swish past, swish past, buildings illuminated against the evening reds and purples.

Further north we ventured, steady rhythm of the road, entering Manchester, New Hampshire, and I still staring out the window. Three large radio towers just beside the highway—tall, red lights blinking, blinking. I imagined a giant Kong-like ape swinging back and forth (no idea why, the image just came to me), back and forth. Our car passed the towers and continued on its trek, but the ape continued swinging from tower to tower in my mind. The latter part of the eventual story, involving the woman Kimberly, is the very scene which played out in my head. Bizarre, but it passed the time.

It passed the time.

Snap! You are awake again, and it's sixteen years later. I had always wanted to write this story, it's characters and general atmosphere seemed to haunt me at unexpected moments. I thought, however, it would be too weird to attempt. Then one day I discovered that horror isn't only about the expected fears and terrors, the good old well-trodden images. Beautiful and terrifying things can happen when a writer bends the rules, twists reality in a way that's never been done before. I found stories in surreal magazines like *The Silver Web* and *The Urbanite*, and realized—My God! I can write The Monkey on the Towers, after all!

So I did.

The Monkey on the Towers

The monkey appeared on a gray September evening, before the final licks of sunlight fell to the halogen glow of street lamps. No one knew where it came from, nor where it went when it suddenly faded from sight.

On September 16th, just after seven in the evening, an extremely large ape took up residence in the city of Manchester, New Hampshire. It swung back and forth between three radio towers standing alongside Interstate 93. For most of the first few minutes it simply propelled itself around the first tower, using its momentum as a centrifugal impetus away from the framework. It should have spiraled towards the ground, but did not. It moved around and around until, perhaps bored of this, it reached with the other arm towards the center spire. Thus began the repetitive act of swinging between the towers in a silent figure-eight. It took no notice of the increasing spectators along the edge of the highway, their automobiles abandoned and forgotten. On the ground below, people kept their distance, feeling more secure behind the white maintenance building a hundred yards away.

Within an hour the interstate was a mass of dented and steaming cars, crushed by the chain reaction from those too far back to notice the spectacle, blanketed by the klaxon of a hundred car horns screaming for attention. Some of the spectators, still reeling from the impact from drivers behind them or to those in front, eventually forgot their wounds and stared at the scene alongside the road.

The ape was large. Too large, according to zoologists interviewed in the months which followed. If the animal were to stand upright, it would have risen half as tall as the towers themselves. It couldn't be classified as any species of primate previously encountered. It was just too big, too surreal in its silent orbit above the ever-growing masses.

By eight o'clock the world around the radio towers was ablaze in light. Police barricaded the area with yellow ribbon. Evening news reporters shoved each other for the best vantage, beaming the creature's image into every household. The monkey paid no heed to the carnival of lights and sounds. It just swept its half-circles around the towers, one massive arm after another.

Two deaths were directly caused by the visitor. The rest resulted from injuries sustained on the highway and from a man who arrived later sporting an AK-47 rifle and what some described as a "joyously psychotic" expression. Of the two deaths caused by the ape, the first happened twenty minutes past eight o'clock.

*   *   *   *

David Pratchett was still in his office when the call rang in from the state police barracks. Within minutes the helicopter, already en route when the veterinarian answered his phone, landed in the grazing fields of the zoo's neglected backland. He watched it land from his office window, the phone still held to his ear.

Now, standing just inside the yellow tape, Pratchett stared up at the animal. He followed its liquid movement back and forth among the towers' few remaining beacon lights. As it did with everyone else, the ape ignored him. Almost. When Pratchett took his first tentative steps away from the barricade, the large expressionless head turned in his direction.

Pratchett stopped. The ape ignored him once more.

"You need to keep these people as far back as possible," he said.

The reply that came into Brian Sullivan's head was quickly suppressed. Instead, the police sergeant said, "We're trying, Mister Pratchett. It's not as easy as it sounds. Everyone's just about hypnotized by this thing."

"This thing…" Pratchett said, considering the words carefully. When Sullivan turned to look for breaches in the fluttering yellow ribbon, Pratchett walked to his death.

"You know we're here," the veterinarian whispered, taking short but deliberate steps towards the center tower. "Are you waiting for something?" The ape crossed over the gaps, curled around and settled into its earlier rotation around a single purchase, the center tower. Around and around, keeping its black eyes fixed on Pratchett each time its orbit brought the man in sight.

With well-practiced calm, Pratchett continued speaking. "It's OK. I'm a friend. Where do you come from?" Lower and lower the creature swung, the free arm curled against its chest. Because of this, Pratchett misjudged its reach.

Sullivan's stomach wrenched when he turned and saw Pratchett's slow advance. "What the hell are you doing?"

The ape's free arm, now fully extended, swung around. In the last second of his life Pratchett saw the giant fist, and thought of Hans Brinker. Remembered reading about the heavy wrecking ball hurtling towards the boy's father. The impact sent Pratchett's shattered body sailing over the white maintenance building.

Seconds of numb silence. The ape resumed its circumnavigation of the towers, around the last, back towards center, moving higher as it did so. Like passengers on a roller coaster, the crowd exploded in a chorus of screams.

"Don't shoot it. Don't shoot it, God damn you." Sullivan pushed Bennie Powers' arms down. The sergeant looked around. "OK!" He tried to keep the screaming out of his own voice and prayed that the trooper wouldn't shoot him in the foot. "Anyone else attempting to cross this line will be arrested. Is that clear?" Then to Powers in a softer voice, "Tell everyone to keep their pieces holstered. Shoot that thing and God knows what'll happen."

*   *   *   *

Kimberly Hobson pulled at the collar of her sweater. The act stretched the fabric beyond returning. Muscles under her shoulder blade tensed and relaxed, tensed and relaxed, in time with the rhythmic movements of the animal on the television. Prime time had been preempted by local news, but only temporarily. The set was now tuned to the New England cable news station, covering the events "as they happened." For Kimberly, the world around the set faded to a blur. She stared at the monkey, watched its oversized muscular frame moving between the towers. When the camera panned across the crowd, or cut away to various shaky interviews with experts, Kimberly felt a panic, like running out of air too far below the water's surface. These subtle changes in his wife were lost on Tom. He continued clicking away at the computer, mumbling occasionally the facts garnered from the jumbled encyclopedia of the Internet.

"Christ," he said. "Nothing. It could be a silverback, but it's way too big, and there isn't any white on it. Is there?" No answer. He didn't turn around. "There's not a whole lot of stuff out here. The rest of the world either hasn't noticed or no one's made any updates. If it wasn't such a madhouse over there I'd go and check it out for myself."

Kimberly heard these last words, and they affected her. She ran fingers across her throat, wondering how far away the towers were. A mile? Two at the most. At that moment the camera image shook. The ape no longer swung but gripped the leftmost tower with both arms and legs. It stared directly into the camera. In the background, spectators squealed nervously.

"Now what?" Tom stood behind her. His voice startled Kimberly from her reverie. He didn't notice. "Oh, man. It's going to attack."

It didn't attack. Staring into the camera which broadcast its image into Kimberly's mind, the animal stretched out one arm, as if pleading an unseen keeper for food, or company.

Tom took an unconscious step backwards. "Looks like it's trying to say something. Maybe it's scared."

Kimberly suddenly found herself standing before the towers. Silence all around. The ape reached down, inviting. Arousal filled her, warm, breathless. She stepped into the open hand. It closed gently, entombing her. The rough palm pressed against her face. No panic. She tried to breathe through the ever-tightening grip.

"What the hell are you doing?" The living room returned with its light and flickering television. Kimberly gasped, laying on her back on the floor. Tom hesitated a moment, then lifted her into the chair. "Are you all right? It looked like you fainted. The hell with this." He reached over and clicked off the set.

"No! Please, don't." She reached for the button. Tom stopped her.

"Kim, what's wrong?"

She closed her eyes, tried to resurrect the feel of the giant hand around her. "Nothing," she whispered. "The news. Everything. I need to lie down."

* * * *

The bed was cold and inviting. Maybe she was too sensitive. Sleep. Better.

Tom turned off the light and closed the door without speaking. Kimberly remained on the bed, eyes open. The earlier fatigue lifted in the solitude. She had to go. Now.

Naked. Her sweater and jeans in a pile by the door. The white dress fell from its hanger and slid over her. She wore nothing else. Cool cotton against skin. Subtly, softly erotic. She put on a thin pair of slippers and left the bedroom. Tom's back was silhouetted against the ever-changing images on the computer. He never turned around, never understood she was gone until it was too late to do anything about it.

* * * *

Nicholas tapped the syringe twice to free the bubbles. Only a half dose, but it should make the monkey go away. Tap tap again. No bubbles. Now the needle was in his arm. Slow push of the plunger. Hot metal in his blood. Thinning. The yellow walls of the apartment dripped and peeled then everything was blue. Pink. Ecstasy. He turned his head, at least he thought he did. The television wore a top hat. Skinny arms (one held a cane) on each side of the square box. It danced about the room. Mickey Mouse just kept jumping up and down on the screen.

Nicholas laughed as he lay on the thin rug. Above the holes in the knees of his camouflage pants, a slow, dark urine stain crept. The television was still on. The news broadcast showed the ape stopping on the leftmost tower, reaching for something unseen before it. Nicholas didn't see this. In fact he was staring at the ceiling. He smiled half from the euphoria and half from the lack of facial control caused by the drug. Just the free-based blissful haze of his universe. The smile tightened suddenly. A frown.

The crash came too early. Purple was here now. The walls solidified, bright evil violet. They breathed, folded in, breathed, twisted out. The room writhed and turned.

"Too soon," he muttered. Crawling to his knees he grabbed the discarded syringe. Still a lot left. He messed up. Just take more. He never got the chance. The wall before him twisted into the head of the ape. It's expression was not blank as on television. It bared teeth, purple like the wall. The eyes complete blackness. It opened its mouth and roared. The sound flooded the room with a physical resonance that buckled the other walls. Nicholas gripped his head. The sound banged inside his skull. Roar. Roar.

"Stop it! Stop it, demon! Satan!" Emerging on either side of the sneering ape-head, two arms stretched forward. One massive fist slammed down beside him. The floorboards split. Nicholas rolled away, landed against the couch. Fingers like tree limbs opened for him.

The weapon was in his bedroom. He sidestepped and ran. Before he reached the doorway the tip of the monster's fingers brushed his back. The darkness of the bedroom rolled under him. He landed on the edge of the mattress, then squatted into a defensive posture on the floor.

The ape's gargantuan head filled the door's frame. The mouth twisted with another angry shout. Everything twisted in response. Reality buckling under the nightmare. Nicholas reached under the bed. It was there. Unfold the blanket. Check the clip. Everything an instinctive motion. No clip. Another roar. Something lifted the end of the bed.

Nicholas whispered, "C'mon.... Where the fuck are—yes!" The clip rolled out of the blanket and into his lap. Slap it in. Roll. Aim.

No sound. The bed crashed to the floor. Nicholas' finger cocked the trigger halfway. He wanted to spray the room blindly and decimate everything in front of him. He did not. Do not fire without the target in view. Don't kill your own men out of fear.

The rectangle of light from the living room was deserted. It must have seen the rifle. Nicholas moved in jerky motions, stopping beside the doorway. The weapon was light in his arms. Adrenaline. Makes a man stronger. Time to move in.

In silence he dove into the light. Roll away. Weapon raised the instant he righted himself.

Nothing. The intruder was gone. Intruder. The left corner of his mouth twitched. Monster. The monster was gone. Nicholas breathed quickly, not wanting the rush to drop into the crash he knew waited. Bad trip. Bad trip. That's all.

On the television screen, the unnatural bulk of the ape returned to its steady rotation around the towers. When Nicholas saw it, he knew it was not a trip.

*   *   *   *

"Return to your home, ma'am." The trooper kept both arms folded across his chest, a solid human wall. Kimberly glanced at the other two policemen. One stood at the opposite end of the barricade, the third tried to convince the driver of a blue mini-van to turn around.

Kimberly said, "I don't have a car." She knew that made no sense. Her voice had the whispering lilt of a madwoman. It didn't matter. She felt more peaceful than she ever remembered and didn't want to lose it. Like hanging on to sleep while closing the windows against a midnight rain.

"Do you live around here?" the trooper asked.

"Just a couple of houses back," she lied.

The man nodded. "Please return to your home, ma'am." It was a mantra he'd likely be repeating the entire night. Some of her inner calm dissipated. She looked down, then back along the road behind her. Quiet, tree-lined street. Middle class homes painted white. A suburban utopia sitting only five miles east of downtown Manchester.

"Maybe I should go." She said it to herself more than to the trooper, who gave no response.

The further down the road she walked, the more people she passed going the other way. *Up the down stair case*, she mused. "They won't let you pass," she said to one person. Either the man didn't hear or she'd spoken the words only in her mind. Either way, she was not important in the lives of these people. Kimberly stopped in front of a darkened colonial and leaned on the fence. *What's wrong with me? Where's Tom?*

She remembered the hand, large, suffocating in its embrace. Trying to breath against its palm. Arousal at the memory of her body pressed further and further inward. It was waiting for her. She needed to get to it. She ran through the darkened yard of the colonial and disappeared into the woods beyond.

* * * *

It was dark between the trees but Kimberly knew that if she kept in the same direction, she'd come out somewhere near the towers. She was past the road block. They were too busy with the beaten-path travelers to think of looking her way. Maybe they didn't care. She sensed there was at least one other person behind her. No fear. She would be safe. Just keep walking. It was close. The ape's presence reached through the dark shadows, pulling her along.

* * * *

Every couple of minutes Nicholas checked the rifle strapped to his back. It was tight against him, but situated so he could swing it ready when the time came. His heart beat with the caffeine of adrenaline. The woman hadn't noticed him, and she wouldn't. No one would. Nicholas Ecklesbury was too well-trained. It'd been decades since he'd concealed himself fully-armed through the woods, but no matter. The act came as naturally as shitting. His eyes tracked the white blur like some surreal beacon, knowing the woman was moving in the right direction. He needed to hurry. The monster had to die soon.

* * * *

She remembered letting Tom hold both her hands in his. She remembered thinking that her dress needed to come off soon, not because of any sexual urge but to rid herself of the starched seam that incessantly dug into her back. When the priest made the official pronouncement of their marriage, a thought occurred to her which lingered in her memory. *I'm married.* As the two bent to kiss, her lips dry as they pressed into his Kimberly thought, *Now what do I do?*

A branch slapped her face. She stumbled backward and fell, face stinging. The monkey's hand wrapped tighter around her. Kimberly took in a breath, wondering if she could ever exhale. She did, and rose to her feet. A hundred yards ahead, lights like stars blinked between wind-blown branches. She saw an occasional figure in the wood fading in and out of the light. They paid her no heed, moving as she now did towards the glow ahead. Earth-laden moths struggling forward, pushed by a blind instinctual urge. A twig snapped. Someone was close behind. She didn't look back, but kept her eyes on the flashing trees.

The honeymoon was in Hawaii. The warm water wrapped around her body. The chartered boat advertised the freedom to swim naturally (a safer word for 'naked'). Kimberly, clothes on the port-side bench, was in the water before Tom had his shoes off. Blurred figures bobbed around her. Too close. She swam out further. Below, the bay darkened to a soft, green opaqueness. They were moored far from the corral reefs to keep others from choosing this spot. Nevertheless, large colorful fish appeared as if from a heavy fog. They circled and inspected her. Kimberly followed one as it swam down. Perhaps, if she followed it far enough, a new fantastic world of color and light would open before her, bright cities hidden below the sun's reach.

Too far. The glittering surface of the water like spilled mercury, out of reach but brilliant in its motion. Too far. She paddled and kicked, the exertion expanding her lungs. Any moment they would explode. With every stretch of arm it seemed her fingers would shatter the surface. With each stretch, the distance became too clear. Bubbles drifted ahead, carrying her life away forever. She stopped swimming, tried to grab the globes of air with her fingers. Drifting down. Tom's naked body, arms under her shoulders. There were no bubbles left to escape. His hand over her face, water racing into her mouth from the canyons etching his palm. Too late. *I've left you.* The fog swallowed her. She awoke, vomiting salt water across the bow of the chartered boat. Never since could she decide whether those final sensations as she sank, or the painful realities of the boat's deck, were the actual hallucinations in death. But the deck was cold and real. Life-giving.

The final tree fell away behind her. Crowds. Cars and police and men and women, in bathrobes and uniforms and suits. Lights shone across the muddy bog of bodies, into each other's eyes, across the massive, swinging body of the monkey on the towers. She stepped into the throng, moving ahead as if each human around her was no more than a tree branch, or a multicolored fish.

A tall, black policeman looked at her, obviously preparing to recite the standard "go home" song. Behind his head, less than fifty yards away, the preternatural ape swung tower to tower. The head pivoted with the grace of a trapeze, keeping its gaze on her. The expression neutral.

"Excuse me, ma'am…" the officer began.

Stop. The command came not from the police officer but from every pore in her body. She stopped.

*　　*　　*　　*

The demon was massive, much more than he expected from the images on the television. Nicholas felt a surge of joy. Yes, this was his mission. His life until now was only a vehicle carrying him to this moment. The monster *was* such only to him. To the rest it was a God. Deceiver. The vision in the apartment showed the truth. A message from the True Creator. The world was in peril, prostrating itself before the Beast.

The woman was his unwitting shield, the first thing anyone would notice as the couple emerged from the woods. Now he sidled off three steps to her right. Swinging the rifle from his back, he raised its barrel towards the heads and backs of the human wall. Do not fire. Not until the path between your weapon and the enemy is clear. Someone grabbed his shoulder, released it just as quickly. The wall parted in screams as one then another saw the assault rifle and the blinded glow on the face of its owner.

The path was clear. Nicholas squeezed the trigger.

※　　※　　※　　※

Go.

Kimberly stepped forward. The officer moved out of the way. He began shouting at someone behind her. Something popped and cracked. Her world filled with the ape. It no longer traveled the figure eight above the crowd, but swung its dark body by one arm and one foot around and around the tower before her. Now and then something buffeted against its body, an almost imperceptible reaction. Was someone throwing rocks?

The monkey kept swinging, around and around, lower and lower. The free arm extended away from it like the whirling spindle of a carnival ride. She was ten feet away. Eight feet. The wrinkled palm was open, more inviting than the mental images drawing her here. It offered the quilted comfort of home. As she stepped across the final distance, she opened then let fall the white dress. She moved naked onto the grass where the massive hand had just passed. She watched it circle away, knowing it would come again. An arousal, more deep and wet than in her most lurid of dreams, floated within her. She took in a breath and did not exhale. The hand came around, raced towards her above the grass.

※　　※　　※　　※

Sullivan moved in unison with a hundred other police officers toward the gunman. He couldn't risk firing without hitting a screaming civilian. A man with a news camera stepped in front of him. Sullivan slammed into him, then walked over both man and camera without breaking stride. He shouted for everyone to get down, but the words only saturated the air with a hundred other voices. The madman continued shooting towards the ape. From a quick glance Sullivan saw some rounds hit their mark. Most passed over the target as the creature lowered itself to ground level. The stray bullets landed in the faces of police and spectators lining the highway.

Less than two yards from the shooter Bennie Powers held his own weapon level with the man's head, shouting as uselessly as Sullivan. Just then the absurd smile on the madman's face twisted into a grimace of rage. Both Sullivan and Powers understood what was coming next and caution didn't play into things anymore. The lunatic was about to fire into the crowd.

"Wake up!" The shooter yelled. "I'll wake y-" One side of his head exploded with the impact of Powers' bullet. The half-decapitated body squeezed the trigger for a moment, sending three rounds into the chest of a prostrate reporter.

With the perfect timing of an hysterical crowd, everyone fell to the ground in time with the shooter's body. Sullivan dropped to one knee, not wanting to lose his line of sight in case there was another madman waiting. It was then that he and a handful of others saw the naked woman standing at the base of the tower.

From head to knees the beast's hand closed around the woman's pale figure. The momentum of such a weight, plus what looked like the sudden, tight squeezing of the fingers, liquefied her body. It was the only word Sullivan could think of, either at that moment or later in his report. From every crack and orifice in the tight ball of the ape's hand came red and cream-colored bile. The lower portion of her legs dragged across the ground in motion with the animal's swing. One thin slipper broke free and tumbled away. As if merely squishing a bug, the ape casually wiped its now-open palm against the grass. The circular trail, wiped carefully and methodically around the tower, resembled nothing of the woman aside from the disembodied calves.

Sullivan's finger pulled the trigger. After the second shot, others joined in. Angry and desperate from their impotence to stop the madman sooner they sent round after round into the ape. Those bullets missing the mark landed in explosions of dust in the hillside beyond. Just as quickly, the shooting stopped. The monkey had raised itself higher on its steel-girded tree.

Black hair glistening with what might have been rivulets of blood, it moved slowly, deliberately to the top of one tower. The narrow peak screamed from the sudden weight, then started to bend. Toes gripping the crisscrossed supports, the ape extended its arms in a crucifixion parody. It stood for a moment above the faces of those screaming, dying, or nervously silent. Black eyes blinked once. The ape fell forward like the Hollywood icon it would forever be associated with.

Sounds of a hundred sudden gasps. Perceived weight falling into the throes of tripping, squirming bodies. Then nothing. No nightmare monkey. One moment it existed in their world, the next it did not. It simply disappeared. The only impact was the silent acknowledgment that nothing more would happen that night.

*   *   *   *

Tom stared at the bed. The light from the living room fell across rumpled, vacant sheets. Behind him, the news anchor repeated his report of the mysterious woman, her death, and the sudden disappearance of the monkey on the towers.

Tom turned, walked past the computer, and sat slowly on the couch. A discarded candy wrapper crinkled beneath him. He felt the wrapper through his pants, saw with slowly emerging clarity the disarray of his house. Alone. The reality, the inevitable truth of his wife's death sank into him, like a lost treasure over the side of the boat.

About "Feed The Birds"

We come now to the first original story in this collection. *Original* meaning it's newly written, and previously unpublished. I had to save it from a year-long wait in the slush pile of an anthology so I could include it here.

I can't say a lot about this story without giving too much away, except that I came up with it while standing in the kitchen looking across the house to the bird feeders we'd established outside the windows. Seeing the happy birdies flutter about, I wondered…well, when you read the story you'll know what I wondered.

No, I don't know why I think these things sometimes. I really don't.

But, between you and me, I'm really glad I do.

Feed the Birds

As usual for a Friday, Doctor John and Doctor Regina arrive home within minutes of each other.

Regina waits beside the garage, tries to concentrate. John ducks below the lowering door and embraces his wife. Regina pulls away, pecks her husband's cheek. The weight of the past five days wears her down. He knows it, feels it himself. Both see in the other's eyes their lassitude reflected. They turn, hands loosely clasped, and walk into the Tudor's side entrance.

Regina whispers, "We have to feed the birds."

Empty plastic bird feeders swing in the breeze beside the row of hemlock lining the driveway. The feeders knock lightly against the house front, calling those inside, wanting to be filled. In the green of the trees beyond, one or two birds have alighted, lost from sight among the leaves. They sing songs and wait. It is not yet time.

The kitchen is large. Dark wood beams soar over contrasting white walls. As Regina walks across the room her eyes scan the counter, toaster, microwave, never resting long on any object. She is distracted and tired. Her briefcase stands on the breakfast table. The coffeemaker hisses and coughs. Half decaf, half regular, the timer set that morning to be ready for them when they arrived. Black steam welcomes senses which are crinkling at the edges, chipping like old paint. Regina inhales deeply, knowing she cannot drink even when it is done.

Minutes later, husband and wife hold coffee mugs with both hands as if warming fingers on a cold day. John lifts the cup to his face. Steam fills his nostrils. He wants to drink its hot, cleansing pain. Not yet. The birds need to be fed, and he isn't yet hungry. The coffee mug is lowered. John stares across the kitchen and sees the past week's faces—crying, screaming, laughing, silent. They parade by, revolving on an invisible spindle.

Eight Years Old, remembers Doctor John. What had the boy seen? Parents whispering, muffled crying, when Eight Year Old pushed open their door, "but my head was being pulled back, down the hall, like a rope coming out of my neck." The boy was describing his instincts taking over as he opened the door, knowing at a base level what he'd see in his parents' room. Something monstrous laid out before him. "Wet and splashy," Eight Year Old says. The boy occasionally devises alternative words to describe the contents of that room. When this happens, John usually finds himself wishing for "wet and splashy".

Each session John takes upon himself these images, holds them close until they no longer threaten the child. Eight Year Old always feels better, while John's stomach burns with their pain. The heat soon fades, only to flare again on Friday afternoons.

Husband and wife, now lost in their memories, sit at the table. The kitchen is silent save an occasional sigh of a shoe against tile.

In memory, feeling her empathy of the week solidify inside her, Regina hears the whispered confessions of Brad Renelle, 10:15 appointment Tuesday. Renelle's hands droop between thighs, fingers interlocked then loosened, chasing each other across the chasm of his legs. His eyes downcast, staring at his shoe, one foot half-out of its loafer, lips wet. Brad Renelle, large imposing man, whispers an obscene confession of his latest fantasy, occasionally glancing up to see if Regina acknowledges his insanity. Is this simple clarity of thought, she would wonder, something good rather than depraved? Always careful is

Regina, never flinching her expression. Never knowing what might set him off. Set *any* of them off.

"We need to fill the bird feeders," Regina now whispers to her husband. Her voice is paper. She licks her lips, tries to swallow. "Before it gets dark."

John lifts his head. Outside the day is still bright with the sideways slant of early summer evening. A dinner appointment tonight with Merrimack Hospital's director of psychology, written on the refrigerator calendar. An Important Man wanting to pull an Important Couple from the warm shadows of their practices. Imprison them in a menagerie of brick and pensions. Plug them in, harness the talent they possess: Doctor John's success rate with children deemed lost, his ability to pull them out of the pit—if only a little higher than anyone one else has been able. Doctor Regina for her papers on adult sexual discord, her radical approaches to violent patients. Men and women excessive in their debauchery, serving extended jail sentences, held far from the community's reaching hands. Her ability to understand the darkness inside them, then extract it. Change them. Sometimes forever. Sometimes for only a week.

The successful couple trudge outside, slowly, like penitent monks with gazes lowered, heading for the feeders in the front. Husband and wife who take upon themselves the filth and pain of children and violent screamers-who-once-were-human. They help their patients secrete from deep within themselves their nightmares and fantasies, tapped like sap into the dented tin buckets of the doctors' souls.

Come unto me all who are weak and heavy laden, and I will give you rest, reads the sign on the wall, in a never-looked at corner of her office. She is beaten, stray dog skittish. But her patients are once again brighter and clearer of mind.

John and Regina move by instinct and routine. They smell the fresh coffee aroma drifting from the open windows, pushing them on with promises of future lightness and taste. One or the other repeats that they have to feed the birds. Zombies in elegantly disheveled business suits, stepping up the driveway onto the clipped grass lawn.

The birds chitter loudly. There are more of them, monochromatic, reds and blues, greens and yellows. Their excitement is audible, watching the couple arrive.

John thinks about Lisa who turned eleven last week. Freckled and tousle-haired, she fights with her right arm which creeps up on her at night, crawling spider-like to her throat when she dares fall asleep.

The low sun hits him in the face. John cannot see the birds but hears them. They gossip and worry. He takes one tube-shaped feeder into uncertain hands. Flashes of blue among the leaves. John fumbles to open the top, sees reds bouncing in the corner of his vision. He remembers angry-eyed Michela who kills every pet her parents bring home, and now her mother is pregnant. John's stomach burns with their fear.

Regina lifts the second feeder from the pole. Tiny screams fall from the trees as if Autumn is early and the leaves have found a voice. The sound tightens her skin. Intense are the creatures' wants and needs, like the bleached woman yesterday who sat in silence for twenty minutes only to skulk to the display case by the window and slam her fist through the glass. In a blink she had dragged the underside of one arm sideways, filling the small transparent box with blood. Regina's stomach cramps with the ice of such blind rage, *their* rage, all of them. The birdsong loops through her head. Chirping, screaming, laughing among the green tree shade. Her stomach is a bag of frozen slush.

John doubles over. Fire in his stomach and throat, liquid molten pain. He thinks of the new boy who started sessions Monday, curled up on the couch and slowly gnawing his fingertips off. John feels the boy in him now, struggling to be set free. Doctor John's mouth closes over the top of the feeder, as does his wife's over the other. He sees her crying, but she is blurred from his vision. The boy on the couch had pulled chunks of skin free before John realized what he was up to.

Now, the boy leaps forward within him, clawing higher, shouting *Let me out*.

The ice cracks into jagged spikes in Regina's stomach. It constricts and conforms to the shape of her esophagus. Like a gush of coagulated oil, black bile curls from her mouth and into the plastic feeder tube. *I am heavy laden*, she thinks. Regina cannot breathe, like when she was young and had the flu, locked in dry heaves, certain she would never breathe again. It's like that at this moment, waiting to die, feeling the man on Wednesday who had shoved a steak knife into his lover's eye now pour out of her in a surreal birth.

To John it feels like a tongue of magma burning from his throat. Then it's out. Cooling. He can breath again. The boy curled on the couch in his office fades away. The torment, sin and disease of the week passes with a few remnant pieces spit into the tube.

Regina does not think any more about the people who should be burned alive, who leave her office feeling freer than before, freer than they should. For Regina, there is only this joyous moment of breathing. So much air inside her, around her for the taking.

The black tar stretches the limits of the plastic housings—frosting one feeder, steaming to translucence the other. Above them the screams in the trees soar to a deafening crescendo. Greens, blues, yellows dart among the branches. High-pitched whistles drop suddenly to deep-throated impatience. The tiny demons take flight.

John is caught unprepared and sees them clearly. He wishes he hadn't, feels close to dying at the consideration of their existence. He pulls his wife away with quick steps and firm grip. She does not resist, taking the summer evening coolness into her lungs. The sky above and around them is fraught with the wings of small bodies, asexual and naked, chittering in hunger and anger. *Out of my way*, John muses the sounds are saying to them. *Let us feed on what you have given back to us*.

John and Regina walk unsteadily along the driveway. Before the corner of the house blocks her view Regina gives in to temptation and looks over her husband's shoulder. The feeders are covered in swarming colors. She focuses on one, a small blue with narrow face. Its wings spread and flutter as it eats. A shorter, yellow demon knocks the blue's wing aside. Above them, gripping one of the protruding metal bars with curved talons, a green man-shape holds in its fist a wad of steaming mucus. It buries its face into some child's sin.

Before the house obscures her view Regina wonders what human blemish it is devouring.

* * * *

They are inside now. Stillness becomes calm.

The kitchen is darkened from the drawn window shade, the feeding outside dancing shadows upon it. John succumbs to the thick coffee smell and lifts the cup to his lips. Though he is shaken, he feels a welcome lightness and tries to recall the details of the past week. All of it remembered, but when he searches for empathy, the pain built with every confession and diverted stare, there is nothing.

Standing in the dim-lighted kitchen sipping from his mug, John knows he is free. Eventually the shadows outside flutter away. Regina is empty, free as well to be only herself. For the weekend. Until Monday, when it will start all over again. Doctor Regina and her beloved husband will open their souls and become vessels into which their patients shall pour their pain and sins. The world expects nothing less of its caretakers. Nor do the demons, which will always return. They will alight upon the trees even when the leaves have gone and the snow contrasts their skin, dimmed in the cold to subtle pastels and gray. They will come, expecting to be fed.

About "The Doll Wagon"

In the summer of 2000, while playing softball during an annual writer's conference called NECON, I struck up a conversation with two other writers: Suzanne Donahue and Stefano Donati. Come to find out each of us had stories slated to appear in the same issue of a horror magazine which never materialized—it went out of business. Suzanne and Stefano also happened to be editing an upcoming anthology entitled, *Poddities: A Creative Tribute to Jack Finney's Body Snatchers*. They asked if I could write something for them to consider. When I got home and was cutting the lawn (I get most of my story ideas in one of two places: the first is behind the lawnmower, the second I'll save for the introduction of "Ptolemy"), a quiet simple story came to mind.

I wrote "The Doll Wagon" in just over a week—a new personal record. Now, evil dolls aren't exactly new to the horror biz, but this seemed like an interesting take on the idea, and I think it came out as one of my best stories. It garnered some nice recognition in the field, including a number of recommendations for the Bram Stoker Award and an Honorable Mention in the *Year's Best Fantasy & Horror*. That's always a nice thing to see.

The Doll Wagon

The Doll Wagon came on a warm night in July, rattling down Claisdale Avenue at nine o'clock. The sky glowed with a prolonged sunset, shimmering ultramarine between the rustling leaves of Maples and Oak. Claisdale Avenue was quiet, most of the children having run home at the call of their mothers or the switching-on of outside lights. Cars in driveways ticked away the days' heat and living room windows cast the neighborhood in a soft, yellow glow.

"Dolls!" shouted the woman in robes.

She pulled the cart behind her. Wind chimes tinkled. Pale white dolls swung from hooks and loops of string, in time with the turning of the large irregular wheels.

"Dolls!" she called again. Her robes fell behind her, lost in the cart's shadow. Black tousled hair fell across her shoulders, over the robe's unused cowl. She seemed out of time, a peddler from another century lost in this quiet, modern suburb.

Faces peered nervously behind screen doors and over the backs of couches. They watched the pale woman walk slowly down the center of their street.

"Dolls," she called, loudly but with patience. On both sides of her cart, dolls of ages past mingled with those found in the local Toys R

Us. They bounced and swung as if in dance, tiny blue eyes reflecting the window lights as they passed, searching out the faces behind the screens. Looking for a home.

* * * *

"I see one! I see one!" Megan was out the door before her mother could react.

Joanne hesitated, screen door held open, and watched her daughter run across the lawn towards the wagon. "Meg, come back here," she shouted, but her call was without heart.

The wagon stopped. Its burden swung like living tassels. Joanne walked quickly down the two front steps and across the grass, following her daughter's path. The woman in the robes knelt before Megan and smiled, reached up to where the little girl pointed, and handed her a chubby baby doll. Its skin matched that of the woman, shiny in the dim light.

As Joanne approached, she saw her neighbors at the edge of her vision. They moved cautiously over lawns, led by their children.

* * * *

"I'm going to call her Megan," Megan said joyfully. William pulled the covers tight under her chin and that of her new doll.

"But that's your name," he said.

Megan pulled the doll out from the covers and held it aloft. The toy face peered down, back into her own. "That's why it's a good name," she said. Her voice had already taken on its pre-sleep sigh. William smiled and kissed his daughter on the cheek. He moved as Joanne came to the bedside.

"Good night, Megan," she said after her own kiss. Her daughter whispered her good night, never taking her eyes from the other Megan.

Joanne stood back and watched the girl slowly lower her arms until the doll rested on her chest and nuzzled under her chin.

*   *   *   *

"You're sure you checked it out?" Joanne lifted the pot of decaf from the coffee maker. A late drop fizzled on the heating unit. "Nothing inside? And you washed the skin?"

William leaned on the edge of the sink and lightly played with his wife's hair.

"Yes," he said. "I promise. I didn't rip the dolls' head off but I squeezed the body and its little legs and arms," he moved his hands in a pantomime of his earlier search. "Nothing."

"Still, all of this is too weird."

William returned his hand to Joanne's hair. "I have to agree with you there. By the looks of the crowd, though, it's a great idea. I mean, hell, when you came back inside I saw more people walking out across the street." He looked past the kitchen towards the living room and added, "Kind of reminds me of when the ice cream truck comes by."

Joanne didn't reply at first, merely took a tentative sip of coffee and wandered towards the front door. William followed her and together they gazed into the street. The wagon, and its driver, had long moved on.

*   *   *   *

The Doll Wagon returned the following night. The air was humid and thick with mosquitoes, more oppressive than the previous evening. She rolled the cart down Claisdale at nine o'clock, calling, "Dolls," in her loud but undemanding tone.

* * * *

"But I want to get one for you!" Megan bunched her fists and stood defiantly in front of her mother. Joanne kept her hand on the door handle and tried to look stern.

"Megan, I understand this is an exciting thing, but you're not taking care of the doll we bought you last night. It wasn't even in your bed this morning."

"I take care of it. It just fell behind something. PLEASE. There were some really nice ones out there, and it's almost your birthday, and there were so many pretty things in there, and oh Mommy, please just one more…"

"Dolls!" called the woman in the robes. The tinkling, swinging cart passed gradually by their house. Joanne turned from her daughter and looked outside. As many people hurried towards the cart tonight as before. Mothers or fathers, pulled along by excited children. Some of them, if Joanne could tell through the cross-hatched screen and dim street lights, looked as worried as she. No one had seen this woman before, and now here was the wagon two days in a row.

Joanne looked down at her daughter and knew any further argument would be fruitless. "One more," she whispered. Instead of whooping with joy as Joanne half-expected, Megan only smiled and led her mother by the hand, out across the grass, like so many children were doing on similar lawns along the street.

* * * *

Megan heard the thing talking to her mother, convincing her to buy another doll. She screamed from under the bed, "Mommy! Don't buy one! She's not me! Don't buy one!" Her words never sounded, never made it past Megan's own plastic doll mind. As she had been doing all day, the girl tried moving her arms, turn herself over, but the arms were fixed, immovable. She could think, could feel her skin on the dusty floor. But none of it felt right.

Her head was turned to one side. A chubby, plastic doll arm stretched away, one finger pointing across the room. A tiny mote of dust stretched web-like between Megan's new hand and the floor.

"This isn't my hand," she sobbed. She heard the thing and her mother go outside. Megan wanted to scream again, but knew it wouldn't do any good. No one could hear her. When she cried, no tears fell from her glassy blue eyes.

* * * *

"Coming to bed?" Joanne leaned on the door frame.

William looked up, startled. "What? Oh.... no. Not yet. I want to stay up and watch the news."

Joanne looked at the delicate figurine which Megan had picked out. It leaned against the small clock sitting on top of the television. The doll was a Chinese princess, nine inches high with flowing pastel robes, white-faced with a red dot on each cheek. Joanne had to admit it was stunning. She said, "If having that thing stare at you all night is distracting just drop it down anywhere."

She tried to sound light, but there was a harshness to her voice.

William looked confused for a moment, then smiled. "Oh, the doll? No problem. It's actually kind of pretty."

Joanne shook her head. "Maybe, but it's bizarre. All of this is."

She wanted to say more, wanted to *scream*. Everything about these past two nights buzzed across her skin like electricity. People didn't wander down streets selling dolls, she thought. She'd said as much to William earlier, and to her friend Nancy when the two ran into each other at the store that morning. The robed woman had found her way onto Nancy's street, as well. How that mysterious woman could do both neighborhoods after being so swarmed with customers on Claisdale, Joanne couldn't say. Yet Nancy said she'd come by around nine o'clock. Maybe there were two of them. Jehovah's Witnesses trying a new tactic, perhaps. She'd have to ask Nancy if the cart came by tonight.

Joanne thought all this, but said nothing. William stared transfixed at something on the television. Finally, she said, "Don't be too late," before turning and going to bed.

*   *   *   *

The woman pulled the cart off the road, into the old Mahew Dye Works' shipping and receiving yard. The pavement buckled with roots that had long since pushed their way skyward, reclaiming the air above. Mahew Dye Works had seen few visitors since closing forty years earlier. There it stayed, crumbling, most of the glass in the windows long fallen inward.

Officer John nodded his head as the woman and her cart lumbered by. He'd been stationed at the entrance to "make sure no one trespasses and risks falling through those old, rotten floor boards".

In the trunk of Officer John's cruiser, a G.I. Joe doll wailed and screamed. It tried unsuccessfully to move its muscular arms. Officer John was blind in the darkness of the trunk, while the thing that stole him closed the rusted gate.

The woman in the robes pulled the cart into the half-open door of the receiving area. If someone stood just outside they might, for an instant, see a sharp flash of metal from the interior's darkness. Someone might catch the outline of something large and angular further down, in what was once the Dye Works' main production floor. Any glimpse inside would quickly be lost when the woman walked back to the door and pulled it closed.

* * * *

When he heard Joanne close the bedroom door, William rose from his chair. It felt like he'd been pulled up—as if the eyes of the Chinese princess cast invisible threads, fine but strong, across the room to entwine him. The small painted eyes beckoned. William heeded and stepped forward.

The doll felt heavy when he lifted it. The princess stared, unblinking, and smiled a smile unchanged since William first saw it. But there *was* something different. He tried to understand what as he sank back into the worn cushions.

Megan had bought the doll for her mother, but William felt a possessiveness for it. Invisible, pulling threads wrapped about him. Just the merest sensation, yet he felt his possession reciprocated. The doll, the princess, belonged to him. The pulling continued. William held the doll close, laying her tight against his chest.

The threads wrapped tighter, hugging, pulling the two of them together. William breathed in shallow bursts. For a moment, he thought he heard his daughter shouting from her bedroom. Then he was lost in pleasure.

* * * *

The next night Joanne expected thunder, at the very least a flash of heat lightening. Neither came. The sky simply opened in a deluge of rain, crashing down on Claisdale Avenue. She watched from behind the screen door. The road was dark, silent, the rain broken only by the glow of house lights across the street.

Her friend Nancy either wasn't home or chose not to answer. Three times during the day Joanne tried to call. Today was Saturday. Maybe Nancy had gone on a day trip with Rich and the kids.

The rain kept falling, in time with her spirits.

"Dolls!" came the now-familiar voice, muffled through sheets of water. How could this be happening, Joanne wondered? Who the hell would be stupid enough to come out tonight? She wasn't surprised. The previous nights carried with them an unreal quality. Whether warm, humid, cool or rainy—it didn't matter. There was something else in the mix. A new element which Joanne couldn't grasp, but was there all the same. A metaphorical shadow in the corner of the bedroom that did not exist in daylight.

"Dolls!" Closer now.

Movement across the street. The Phillipsons came outside. They were silent except for Max, the father, who kept insisting they weren't going out into the rain for a damned doll! More words exchanged, lost to the weather and the call of the woman in the robes. The man was pulled excitedly along by his two children. His wife followed, a hand on her husband's shoulder. Joanne wondered if she wasn't, perhaps, pushing him forward.

A man's voice behind Joanne said, "I'd love one of my own."

She let out a cry and spun around. William smiled and touched his wife's shoulder. "A doll, I mean. Who knows how much longer she'll decide to come by?"

Joanne told herself her heart was beating frantically because of her husband's sudden appearance. But there was more. A slow burning in her stomach, a softening in her legs. Joanne was afraid. In the hall leading to the bedrooms, little Megan stood in silence and watched. Joanne looked alternately between the two, and slowly shook her head.

William stroked her shoulder. "Oh, come on. You guys got one. It's only fair." A light tug on her shoulder, barely perceptible, towards the door. Joanne pulled away.

"No," she whispered. Why the hell was she acting like this? Terrified of a doll wagon, or of the dolls themselves? Of the strange woman outside?

Megan walked up and touched her mother's hand. Joanne flinched. Afraid of her own family.

Absurd. She was tired. They hadn't taken a vacation yet. Not enough rest.

"Mommy," Megan whispered. "Can I buy Daddy a doll?"

Joanne wanted to say "no" again, reach out and slam the door and slap her daughter then slap her husband, scream "NO, NO, NO." Lock them all inside. Wait until that damned wagon rolled away.

Instead she wrapped her arms about herself and said nothing. What could she say?

Tears began to well. William didn't notice as he pulled out his wallet and checked the contents. He walked into the rain alone. Joanne listened to his footsteps fade away.

Megan watched her mother, but said nothing more.

* * * *

William shook the rain from his hair with one hand and held the court jester with the other. The doll's outfit was red and blue with bells tinkling from the multi-faceted crown.

Joanne sat on the couch and did not ask to see it. Still, her husband held it before him. "Well?" he said, moving the doll a little and letting the bells jingle. "A nice one, don't you think?"

Softly, their daughter said, "Mommy, he has such pretty eyes."

He did. William held the doll in front of him and stepped slowly, very slowly, toward the couch. Joanne found herself captivated by the tiny blue eyes. They reflected the lamp light, shined all the bluer as William approached. She felt a warmth across her shoulders, as if someone embraced her from behind. Joanne leaned against the sofa as far back as the cushions allowed. Still, the doll loomed closer.

Her tears fell freely now. She sobbed once, but didn't want to frighten Megan, make her think Mommy was losing her mind. The girl moved softly to kneel beside the couch.

"Lay down here, Mommy," she said. Joanne wanted to look away from the court jester, from his white face and jingling bells. Megan touched her sleeve, gently, but it was enough. Joanne slid down until her head rested against the arm of the couch. William held the doll and smiled.

Joanne reached out and took it. The act did not feel voluntarily—more like the doll reaching out for her. William lifted her legs onto the couch. Joanne felt his hands, wet and cold from the rain, on her ankles.

She could run. Joanne knew, somehow, that she could run, close herself somewhere safe. But for how long? This was her family. Could she ever truly run from them?

Megan fumbled with the top two buttons of Joanne's blouse, then gently guided her mother's hands down until the doll rested its hard white face against her mother's skin.

Joanne's body tingled. Her legs shook. She could run, she could run, she could run. She closed her eyes, felt the doll breathing on her neck. Not a physical expulsion of air, rather a presence—a *touching*. The sensation spread. Joanne no longer felt her legs.

*　　*　　*　　*

There came a night when the Doll Wagon rolled down Claisdale Avenue for the last time. Mosquitoes circled the heads of the people as they walked slowly from their homes.

"Dolls…" called the woman in the robes. Her wagon was empty, save for a few strings and hooks swinging freely from their perches, wind chimes tinkling in the breeze. The people came forth, faces obscured in shadow from the house lights behind them. Each held their dolls reverently in both hands. All were silent, save for the voices of the dolls which only the new residents of Claisdale Avenue could hear.

"Please, let me go," some of these voices said.

"Where are you taking us?" said others.

"Mommy!"

"Baby, where are you?"

"I can't see you! Where are you?"

One by one, the dolls were laid upon the wagon's many shelves, or hung from the hooks and loops of string.

William walked to his car and returned with a red gasoline jug. He tilted it and circled the wagon, letting the fuel glug from the yellow spout. In unison the neighbors backed up to watch from their lawns. Finished, William returned to his family.

The woman produced a silver Zippo lighter from her robe, flicked it open and alight, then tossed it burning into the cart. A "whoosh". The wood cracked and blackened. Tiny clothes, nylon hair curled into flame. The people smiled warmly as they watched and listened. The dolls' screams mixed with the smoke, drifting high into the warm summer night.

About "Redemption"

OK, time to be honest. No matter how many times I tried, I just couldn't sell this damned story. Well, that's not quite true. Remember me mentioning in "The Doll Wagon" introduction, how I had a piece accepted for a magazine which eventually went under before the story saw daylight? Well, this was it. It felt great to sell this one, as it had a long and sordid history of revisions and rewrites. When the magazine went under, I just couldn't sell this piece anywhere else. Why? I have no idea! Granted, it might simply be that the story, well, stinks like bad cabbage. I'll let you be the judge, since I'm giving it a home here in my humble little collection. Personally, this story is probably so deep, so profound, that other editors felt it would make every other story look bad.

Right. Well, *I* like it—a lot—so it stays. Hmmpph!

Anyhow, interesting background to this story. When I buckled down a few years ago to do some serious writing, my debut piece of fiction was a nine thousand word epic with a plot so *amazingly* original, that it would catapult me to fame overnight. You see, I'd come up with the idea of writing about an asteroid coming to earth, and very little time remaining to stop it. What would the average person do in those final days? Treat it from their perspective, keeping all the science fiction broo-ha-ha out. Nothing like it had ever been done!

Halfway through writing "Doomsday" two movies were released: "Deep Impact" and "Armageddon". I guess the factual near miss we had with a large asteroid the year prior inspired a lot of other people besides me. Still, I trudged on and finished the piece. It received a lot of attention—in the form of rejection letters.

I cut the story down to six thousand words, then five thousand, boiling it to its essence. Same response. Finally, I canned it, letting it simmer and age like a fine wine. By this time, the story was called "No Redemption by Doomsday." You can see from this that I was getting desperate.

A year later, I resurrected the piece, and read it over. It wasn't as good as I'd remembered. But, there was one minor scene—a nightmare the main character kept having about a beating he'd received the year before. Light dawned! I trashed everything but three things: the dream (which became the primary plot line), the phone conversation with the character's wife which I really liked, and the naked lady. (Gotta keep the naked lady.) It sold, but soon became "available" again (see above note re: *out of business*). I tried remarketing it. Nope. Hmm…I slashed and attacked the prose, tighter and tighter. Sweat poured from my brow, blood smeared the keyboard. Though I began to get some good comments from editors, they were part of an overall "no". Still, you must try and try. Still, "no" and "no". Finally, seeing that I'm putting this collection together, I'm going to make all of you read it whether you want to or not!

Ladies and Gentlemen, I give you "Redemption". Read it. Read it or so help me I'll hunt you down like an animal and *make* you read it!….and you'd better enjoy it….

Redemption

Standing between dream and memory, Jacob Dempsy turned away from the cooler doors. No buying the six pack this time, so unnecessary this late at night. He moved, as if floating, to the front.

The old man behind the counter sniffed. "Will that be it?"

The six pack was in Jacob's hands. He let it go. It faded away, reappeared as the old man dropped it into a brown paper bag.

"I don't want to do this," Jacob whispered. "Just stop." This was a dream, *the* dream. He knew that. Wanted it to change just one time.

The storekeeper whispered, "Can't do that." He took the money Jacob hadn't offered him and flipped the bills into the drawer. He didn't bother to give change, but said, "Just hold on. It'll all be over soon."

Through the window's neon beer sign, Jacob watched three men walk up to his Toyota and lean on the hood. The skinny one, a tattoo of a dragon scrawled on his cheek, waved like an old friend. Even from this distance the animalistic rage swirled like a thunderhead in the man's eyes. Rage directed at Jacob, the car, whatever drove him and his buddies to sit outside this liquor store one year ago and wait to kill a stranger.

In the original run of the drama they failed. But only barely. One of the three, a splotchy Irishman with freckles staining his face and arms, had knocked the bag to the ground as Jacob left the store, then held him from behind while the skinny guy kicked. Jacob's only real memory was the blur of pain, smell of urine and oil as his face pressed against the pavement. A work boot from the third attacker, a fat man in a tight black Harley t-shirt, cracking ribs, working at Jacob's skull. Then, Jacob simply curled up, numb, and waited to die. In subsequent dreams, like the one he found himself in now, gaps in his memory were filled. He felt every impact.

With only vague physical attributes and a generic description of a white Plymouth Fury, the police never made an arrest. Jacob's attackers disappeared from existence. Hiding in his mind was how it felt, cowering in his head like scavengers waiting for nightfall. Until he was asleep, defenseless.

Jacob waited at the door. *Not this time. Not this time.* Still clutching the bag, he turned and walked away. Gravity pulled him down but he waded on towards the back exit. Cracked green floor tiles had an elasticity like in a carnival moon walk. He couldn't breath. The tinkle of a bell as someone came in behind him. Heavy footsteps. A low rumbling like a distant train became the pounding of some monstrous buried machinery.

The back door was chipped red. Jacob pressed the lever. It broke off. Behind him, bottles fell to the floor. A hand slapped his shoulder. Jacob tossed his weight forward, into the door. It opened.

Daylight. Silence. Panoramic hills and distant mountains, never a part of the city's actual landscape, spread away before him now. Cool mountain air. He was free. A shadow covered the hillside. As Jacob turned, something burned from the sky and screamed down on top of him.

* * * *

The baseboard heaters clicked. He turned his head towards the clock. Two-thirty. He waited. Two-thirty-one. Jacob rose from the couch and peered behind the window shade. Some of the windows of other townhouses glowed the iridescent blue of televisions. He wrapped his bathrobe tighter and began his own blue-tinged vigil.

* * * *

Jacob let the words of the newscasts fall across him, recycled forms of the same story. "Tomorrow is Doomsday." And it was too late to do anything about it.

The dream tried to force its way back into his thoughts. He wrestled it away. Dr. Chin was right. Not talking about it, even with Claire, was why the dream kept returning. But he was alive, and if moving on with his life meant having a nightmare once a week, twice a week, so be it. He didn't need to talk. Didn't want to talk.

Muffled sounds outside. A fight. The baseball bat leaned against the table. He lifted it carefully, not wanting to move back too closely to the window. Looting and death spread like the fires that accompanied them. He imagined demons crawling from some new crevice in the world, snatching up souls before the end of everything.

Jacob lay back on the couch, hearing the occasional siren. Over the course of the night the sound came more and more infrequently. Obviously deciding that being with their families this final night on earth was the priority, police and fire crews simply gave up.

He stared at the phone. The chord hung flaccidly over the edge of the table. Claire would call. She *had* to call. Not that it mattered. He could no more get to the airport to meet her than stop the world from falling apart in a few hours. When the first news hit the air two days ago, neither of them believed. She stayed on in San Francisco. One more day and she'd have the sale wrapped up. This afternoon she phoned. Her flight was still scheduled. At that point both knew it may have been too late.

Jacob listened to the fight outside, and dozed.

When the phone rang he snapped awake with the receiver already against his ear. Claire's voice, fighting for attention with the constant hiss of static.

"...and, and I wasn't eligible for the seat, and the people are crazy..."

"Claire? Is that you? Where are you?" He checked the time. Four forty-two.

"Jacob," she said, "there are people and people at the door to this phone. They're trying to get in. I don't even know if I can get out of here...." Her voice trailed off. Jacob listened to her breathing, to the shouting in the background.

"Claire, where exactly are you? I'll try and pick you up—"

"Pick me up? How the hell are you going to do that? I'm in Chicago. They made us get off the plane in Chicago and they're not letting anyone back on. Christ, Jacob, open your fucking ears!"

He closed his eyes.

"Jacob...." The background shouts gained in volume. "Jacob, I'm sorry. I didn't mean that. They're getting the door open."

"Claire—" he wanted to say he loved her, that he always will, some loving phrase that could not reach his lips. She was all he had left. He couldn't even picture the faces of his parents anymore. Only he and Claire, gripping a single electrical life line.

"Claire, are you all right? Claire?"

A series of rapid beeps, then a man's voice said, "Hello? Hello! For Christ sakes..."

Jacob said, "Who is this?"

There was a slight pause, then, "Get off the phone, asshole. You're tying up the line. You had your turn."

"Who the hell is this?"

"Get off the fu—" Jacob hung up.

*   *   *   *

CNN exploded into static fifteen minutes later. Somewhere nearby a window shattered. Jacob gripped the bat tighter in one hand, numbly sipped his last bottle of beer with the other. Liquid flashes of light from the television played across his face. He didn't want to sleep.

*   *   *   *

The old man concentrated on a small roll of lint on his sleeve. Outside, three men shifted uneasily against the car.

They're only parts of a dream. Jacob wanted to believe that. Their uneasiness implied an awareness, as if these figments of his own bedeviled mind remembered how he'd gotten away the last time.

"I need you to call the police."

The old man looked up, then turned his attention back to the lint. "Why should I do that?" he said. "Nothing happening that I need them for."

"You know what's going to happen. Just call."

"Can't do that. Sorry."

Jacob looked around. Through the sputtering neon he saw the men coming towards the door.

He stumbled past an ancient tower of greeting cards and grabbed the door handle. The guy with the dragon tattoo reached for the knob. Jacob twisted the lock.

"Come on now, friend," the man sang through the glass. "Let us in. We just want to purchase some beverages." His two buddies guffawed.

Jacob had no time for this. The world was about to get smashed apart and he was having the same damned dream.

The old man shuffled beside him. "Excuse me, please." Without looking up he reached for the lock and turned it. "We can't be locking this door. These gentlemen have a right to come in, just like you."

Jacob grabbed his arm, tried unsuccessfully to pull it away. The lock twisted open. The door's small bell tinkled as the smiling men walked in.

Jacob wanted to cry. "Why did you do that? Why?"

The old man didn't answer. In his slow gait he moved back to the counter. The skinny man put a hand on Jacob's shoulder.

"Hey, buddy. Long time no—"

"Fuck you." Jacob sent a knee into his crotch. The man doubled over. Immediately the fat guy grabbed Jacob by the shirt.

"That wasn't very nice." He spun him around and shot a fist into his back.

The air in Jacob's lungs crystallized. He fell to the floor. A boot in his ribs. Something cracked inside his chest. By now the skinny man had recovered. He grabbed a bottle of Jack Daniels and held it like a club.

The bell over the door tinkled. Claire stumbled in, her face bruised and swollen. Her jaw dropped open like Marley's ghost. She screamed. For a fleeting moment Jacob felt relief. The police would hear this. The skinny man hurled the bottle at her face.

* * * *

Jacob opened his eyes to darkness. The television was off. So was the clock. His heart hammered in rhythmic panic. Claire's screams wouldn't leave his head. Slowly, gray images from the room came into focus, dull light soaking through the shades. He gripped the bat and stood. The screaming didn't stop. It was coming from outside. Not Claire. The scream choked off for a moment, fell to a sob. Then the woman started in again. From far off someone shouted at her to shut up.

Maybe she was being raped, long-tailed demons gripping her flesh, taking one last thrill. Reluctantly, Jacob walked towards the front door. The bat felt weightless, non-existent. Everything was going to shit outside. Between screams, the woman muttered unintelligible pleas.

He had to do something. He wouldn't just curl up like a baby. Not this time. *They're outside*, he thought. *Don't make the same mistake. This time you don't have to do anything. Just stay here.*

From outside, "Someone help me, please. Someone…" Then silence.

Jacob opened the door, stepped onto the small porch. No one waited against his car. A warm steady wind tore over the buildings, the air too thick and humid for early October. A gust knocked him against the railing as he descended the stairs, bat squeezed in both hands. He rounded the corner of the building.

The naked woman was kneeling on the grass with her back to him. She was alone, staring at the sky. It took Jacob a few seconds, staring first at the woman's tense buttocks then up to the sky, to come to grips with what floated above them.

The eastern sky was a bright white ceiling, slowly overtaking the dimming stars. The monstrosity rose from the horizon, its full outline still out of sight. Morning light along the surface gave definition to uncountable craters marring its landscape. In its completeness, the thing was the glowing face of a monster, a nightmare man in the moon.

The woman tried speaking to the sky, but her voice collapsed into a dry hissing.

Behind him a man said, "That's the most incredible—"

The voice snapped the tentative line holding Jacob together. He didn't think, didn't wait to decide who it could be. Spinning on one heel, he swung the bat. He put every bit of strength he could summon into the already unstoppable momentum. When the bat hit the man's head, Jacob leaned into it. *Hit him hard. One chance.*

The impact sent reverberations up his arms and shoulders. The man's head tilted. His legs collapsed under him and he fell onto the sidewalk, eyes open and bleeding. Jacob had the bat sailing again. It pushed the skull into the concrete. Blood poured over blond hair. A voice deep in the center of Jacob's mind begged him to stop. It was a weak, ineffective plea. He hammered the bat down again, and again. The victim's face looked like a rubber mask, empty, incomplete.

Blood splashed into Jacob's eyes. He blinked, stopped his assault long enough to wipe it away. His fingers smeared red.

The door of unit thirty-one closed. Someone had seen him. Someone watched him kill this man. He blinked away the memory of the face. He'd been one of them. Had to be. Had to be one of them.

"Kill me, too."

The woman's voice behind him was so damaged it sounded artificial. Jacob turned. On her knees she faced him now, her too-pale skin flecked with dots of blood. "Please kill me. I don't want to be here when it comes." She closed her eyes, expecting the maniac in front of her to comply. She mouthed the word "please."

A dark, erotic wave boiled inside him. All he wanted to do was smash the bat down, keep playing this new game, hit them, smash them, beg his buddy for more quarters.

He saw a white Plymouth Fury pass between two buildings. It glided along the drive and disappeared from view.

In a blink, animalistic mind-numbing rage twisted into terror. He had to get inside. Behind him the woman tried unsuccessfully to scream her objections.

Jacob slammed the door, let the baseball bat drop. Outside, the car hissed along the pavement.

Through the curtains he watched it roll past. The car wasn't a Fury. A nervous-looking black woman leaned over the steering wheel, obviously in search of a particular townhouse. She gave no notice to the crushed body of Jacob's next door neighbor. That's who he was. His name was Tom, or Tim. It didn't matter, anymore.

Outside, the world grew brighter. Jacob leaned against the door.

"I'm sorry," he said. In his mind he saw a child's vision of God, flowing white beard falling across his robes. This God looked down at him, the tight angry frown saying all that needed to be said. The image turned away.

Jacob felt the devil clawing through the ground to reach him. The room shook, sending the remote control skidding across the top of the television. The distant rumbling became a roar. He fell to his hands and knees and crawled along the carpet. The world jerked back and forth. The television tube exploded when it hit the floor. Breaking glass in every room. The townhouse was committing suicide.

The earthquake stopped. Above him, the ceiling split. Beams groaned as gravity tried to pull the queen-sized bed through the floor. Jacob didn't move. He lay on his back, staring at the jagged scar above him. *Let it fall*, he thought. *Just let it fall.*

* * * *

Morgan and Sarah Kane ran out of their unit across the street. Above, clouds raced beneath the massive, falling stone. Morgan called his brother's name. Sarah grabbed his arm, but he'd already seen it. His brother lay on the sidewalk across the way. His head didn't look right.

An old woman stumbled, crying, from unit thirty-one. "I'm so sorry for not stopping it," she shouted. "But what could I do? He would've killed me, too."

Morgan looked absently between the old woman and the monstrous rock in the sky. He whispered, "Who killed my brother?" Deep below the cracked street the rumbling began again.

* * * *

The supports split above Jacob's head. He tried to remember a prayer, maybe the "Our Father." Too long away from church. Too late for any redemption.

The quake hit full force as the dead man's brother came through the front door. Jacob recognized him. Then everything imploded around them. Morgan Kane fell forward. His wife struggled through the shattered entrance in pursuit. She begged him to come back, not to let it end like this. She fell into the room. Jacob let himself pretend she was Claire.

Claire coming home.

"You son of a bitch!" The man clambered on top of him. "Wipe that fucking smile off your face."

Hands around his throat. Jacob grabbed the other's arms, but never resisted. This was an angel sent to squeeze penance from him. The grip loosened. The angel couldn't keep his balance. Their figures tumbled across the floor in time with the earth's breakdown. The ceiling sighed, gave out. The dark lumbering shape of the bed loomed like a miniature version of the annihilation outside. When it fell the floor boards twisted and cracked open. It missed them, landing at Jacob's feet, kept on going. The tentative grip on his throat fell away.

For a fleeting moment the shaking stopped. Jacob turned in mid-air, like flying in a dream. He was falling. The floor of the basement seemed to hurl itself up at him.

Black. Then, slow consciousness. Back into chaos.

The broken floor of the basement shifted beneath him. He saw the dark, swirling tempest in the sky above through the jagged remains of the floors.

The earthquake's howling fell to a background hum. The earth took in its final breath. The light outside dimmed.

Jacob tried to roll sideways. Hot, wet pain burned down his back. He touched something protruding from his belly, felt the long wooden stake. A vampire run through the heart. But it missed. Everyone missed. After a too-short respite, the world heaved in its final death throes.

Across the room, the angel bled from a gash running along the middle of his face. He held the woman. Her eyes were open, frightened and unfocused. She stared without blinking at a spot far above. Jacob stumbled forward, feeling the stake pull out of him. He covered only a few feet before rattling plates deep below the floor finally split. His legs dropped into a crevice. Dust and steam. As he slipped into the entrance of hell, Jacob thought he saw the angel rise on a slab of earth, racing skyward as if to meet his destroyer half-way. He carried with him the body of the woman.

Rapture, Jacob thought.

His feet had become wedged into the tight confines of the crevice. No more light above. The walls squeezed in. Jacob felt his feet and legs crush out of existence. He wanted to say the "Our Father." Something large moved up his throat.

No weight. No maddening violence. The sensation of hitting smooth road after miles of torn and grooved pavement. He rose without pain. In the blackness he sensed, then moved through, the asteroid's mass.

Brilliant stars. The earth enormous, looming below as in a proportionally-skewed dream. In its center a dark, scorched growth nuzzled itself below the surface. Dust sailed past the atmosphere into dispassionate space.

From the carnage, a river of souls like his own flowed, converged toward a single expanding star. Its light stretched forward, celestial arms gathering up its children. Jacob watched the tide move with unnatural speed. He felt no motion of his own. The light expanded, outshone the rest of the universe. Jacob swam in it, barely able to see the river spiraling away.

The light blinked out. The other stars returned, their illumination tarnished by the display. Jacob had the unwelcome sensation of falling, back toward the crumbling planet.

*   *   *   *

He opened his eyes. Green tiles. He should have been surprised, should have screamed in defiance.

He wasn't surprised. All so logical to him now. Jacob stood, muscles thick as if replaced with layers of fat. The old man moved around the counter. He stopped at the front door and turned, his voice the only clear sound around them.

"You were so damn close, Jacob." He opened the door and said, "He's all yours," then left the building. The lethargy in Jacob's muscles crawled into his brain.

The skinny man and his two buddies walked in.

"Well, well, Mister Dempsy," he said. "We meet again." The fat one was the last to enter. He seemed to be suffering from the same fatigue as everyone else.

Jacob breathed stale air. "You tricked me."

He watched the fat man lean against the door. The world outside was a pale white. Nothing there. Empty. The walls absorbed the whiteness—the *nothingness*.

"You had your chance," the skinny man said. His eyes darted around the room. The walls were gone, replaced by white.

Jacob fell slowly to his knees, unable to support his own weight. "You thought you could hold me back," he said. "Play this game in my head forever. Like this is Hell or something."

The skinny man forced a smile. "Isn't it? All the others swam away to Heaven. You saw that. Where else *could* we be?"

The fat man was gone. The Irishman dropped against the greeting card stand. A moment later *nothing* washed over that section of the store.

Jacob whispered. "Somehow you got in my head, kept me running, kept on playing this damned game of yours. You drove me crazy. Made me screw up."

The other watched the last of his buddy blink from existence. He took a half step forward. "It worked," he said, looking everywhere except at Jacob. "You…you were a bad boy, Jacob. Now you get to play with us…with me at least, forever…. Ummm.." He pranced back and forth, not certain what to do next.

"It worked great," Jacob breathed. "But we're not in Hell. There is no Hell. You're in the same place you've always been. My mind. But it's fading, now. There was only one place to go when I died, and you fucked it all up."

The skinny man tried to kick him, but the nothingness caught his arm like a bug on fly paper. Still, as his arm and shoulder blended into the advancing wall, he stretched a leg out, tried unsuccessfully to connect with Jacob's head or chest. He screamed without sound, his face twisting in revulsion as it drowned in the white. The remaining arm reached up, as if to grab his own hair and pull free the body. Then nothing. Jacob was alone.

Five feet. Four. Jacob watched the floor shrink like a thin piece of ice. He wondered if this was the end, if he would simply blink away. Maybe something waited on the other side. Maybe not. It didn't matter. In the end, maybe his only redemption was to finally see this nightmare fade away. Forever.

About "Ptolemy"

OK, you've had a couple of heavy stories to suffer through. Time to get weird with a story that I came up with while sitting on the toilet.

Remember in my "Monkey…" discussion I mentioned a couple of magazines that deal exclusively in "surreal fiction"? One was called *The Urbanite*, and it's still around, though published infrequently. *The Urbanite* liked to have theme-issues, and one day while reading the magazine I learned that the next theme was "Zodiac". Hmm, thought I, a surreal story dealing with the Zodiac. I thought of stars, then the constellations, then I had to go to the bathroom.

Sitting upon the Daily Throne, I pondered the constellations (I didn't have any reading material at that moment). What came to me was a strange image of a man standing in his back yard with a spoon. The constellations were pouring out of the night sky *into* this spoon. Well, I had to finish up what I was doing, and thought nothing more about this tale, until I next sat down—to write, that is. I took the scene, and began writing in *stream of consciousness*. That means I wrote whatever came to mind, with only one rule—I wanted twelve sections, one for each of the zodiac signs. There really isn't any relation between the twelve Signs of the Zodiac and what happens in each section, aside from what I might have snuck in during later drafts of the story. I just wanted twelve sections. Call me shallow, go on.

And, here it is.

Ptolemy

I.

Capricorn dripped into the spoon like black syrup. The silver plating sparkled; reflected the stars. Adam lowered his arm, terrified of the act and the thought he might spill. Digging under the grass with his free hand, he lifted a handful of dirt and poured the constellation into the hole.

He replaced the mound of earth. Small stars flowed around the edges as the black ether spread under the weight. Slowly, as if drowning, the pinpoints faded into the backyard. The pure and horrible understanding, which had gripped him ten minutes earlier and sent him running into the house for the spoon and gun, did not abate. Adam cried, seeing in his periphery the remaining stars swirling above, as if gently stirred by the spoon. The utensil was no longer in his hand, however. It lay beside him on the ground, dark, reflecting only the light from the kitchen window.

Adam pushed the revolver's barrel to the roof of his mouth. He pulled the trigger, freeing the flame and smoke into his frightened brain.

II.

"No. I'm sorry."

Camden opened his eyes. The dreamless, swirling vortex of sleep burned away under the harsh glare of sunlight streaming in from the window. He looked around the room, trying to remember. Her leg protruded from behind the couch, tinted blue in the daylight.

He remembered. Mostly. At some scattered point after last night's violence he must have simply lay down on the red-spattered carpet and slept. Why would he do that? Perhaps he'd fainted.

"No. I'm sorry."

The words belonged to the woman. Though she could no longer speak, her nervous, apologetic voice echoed in his skull as if his brain's only remaining thought. Originally spoken last night, before he pushed his way in, intent on salvaging some tattered remnants of pride lost to those three words.

Now, laying on her living room floor, he couldn't even recall the woman's name. Couldn't quite hold on to the reasons for his original obsession.

Camden stood slowly. His hands were still wet. What time was it? He smeared the blood across his tee-shirt.

"No. I'm sorry."

"Shut up," he said. "You're sorry. Fine. I get it. It wouldn't have worked out anyway."

He looked around the small apartment. Though her body was out of sight from his new vantage (had he put her there?...yes, he thought so...), her blood was all over the room. Camden looked despondently at the broken statuette on the rug. His heart seemed to stop, then start, sputtering like a neglected engine.

When he finally found the mobility to turn and leave the apartment, he yelled behind him, "Why did I come here, anyway?" He waited for the elevator. The apartment door hung open. He did not go back. Instead, he let himself be carried down to the basement.

III.

"Get him out of here, now!" As if swatting away bugs, the police sergeant waved at the two EMTs. They remained standing, one at each end of the gurney and its bleeding occupant. They watched the night sky fall, draining like bath water towards a single point in the lawn. The portable flood lights dimmed respectfully to the blinding stars, which twisted and compressed into the earth beside where Adam's body was found.

"Ralph, please! The man's dying, for God's sake."

Ralph looked down. Adam's broken skull was tightly bandaged, but blood still leaked onto the gurney. The EMT made a concerted effort not to look skyward as he lifted one end. The action broke his partner's spell. For the moment they ignored the sight above and carried the bleeding man to the ambulance. Behind them followed Adam's son, home from college the week before and who had been immersed in laundry when his father pulled the trigger.

Ralph hit the emergency lights as he got behind the wheel. His partner and the son secured the gurney in the back as the ambulance pulled out of the driveway. Ralph stared ahead, eyes riveted on the flashes of trees in the headlights.

Standing in the backyard, the police sergeant watched the night sky. From all points, stars drifted and coalesced above him. They crashed down with dizzying size and velocity, contracting into a single brilliant line burrowing without sound or fanfare into the ground at his feet.

Something moved in the grass. The sergeant watched numbly as a garden snake melted into the light, dripping with the cosmos into the dying man's lawn. Below his shoes the ground rippled like water.

IV.

He was hungry. Camden looked up between the cliffs of the buildings. The late morning sky was tinted orange, the constant haze of smog impervious to dispersion, save from the occasional typhoon. He emerged from the alley. The sidewalk was crowded, many people either standing immobile, portable radios pressed to their ears, or looking skyward as if waiting for some divine sign to help them make it to lunch. Camden did not bother contemplating the reasons for their behavior. These people no longer existed in his world, anymore than he in theirs. Like a nagging headache, an inner voice asked why he did it; what he would do now. Camden buried it, mentally grinding the voice into the concrete until, at last, the questions were as dead as his life.

His existence up until now had been pointless. He understood that more than anyone. Throughout the years he held to some vague illusion of hope. Someday he could rise from the ditch he had dug since childhood, change his life. No longer. A wall, eternal in height and thoroughly unscalable, rose in his future. It was the last wall in the maze, too late to realize the path was wrong. In a few minutes the swarm of police, who he imagined were closing in at this very moment, would push him against this wall. Life would end.

He was still hungry. Wong's Diner offered itself before him. The lunchtime horde hadn't crammed themselves through its doors yet. It would have to do.

V.

Adam squeezed his son's hand. Benjamin barely felt it. The siren screamed like professional mourners come a bit too early.

"Why did you do it?"

Keeping his eyes open took too much energy, so the dying man let them fall closed. He thought about the question. Benjamin's grip didn't waver. When he spoke, Adam's voice was no more than a scratch on a blackboard.

"They were right."

Benjamin leaned closer to his father's mouth. "What? What did you say?"

"I have a hole in my head. I made a hole in my head...."

"It's OK. Don't talk. We're almost there."

"We're the center of the universe." He licked his lips, sending a line of blood down his chin. "Everything revolves around—"

One of the monitors beeped wildly, then settled back to a steady rhythm. As the technician checked his father's pulse, Benjamin watched the bandages slowly turn crimson.

"Why isn't he dead?"

The ambulance surged upward like a ship riding a wave. It settled back, on course as before. The technician turned to face the driver. "What the hell was that?"

The ambulance heaved once more. A storm brewed at sea.

Benjamin looked at his father's face. Adam stared back at him.

VI.

The chicken was dry. Camden absently plucked a hair from the skin. Sitting in the darkest corner of the restaurant, he lifted the plate. The yellow place mat sported a circle with elaborate renderings of animals. 'Zodiac' sprawled across the top, the characters almost unreadable, implying a long-lost Asian alphabet. The circle was divided, pie-like, into twelve groups of years. Camden squinted in the dim light, searching for the year of his birth, the beginning of the proverbial line.

"What the hell is it all about?" A question posed not to him but to an invisible expert standing among four or five drunken customers. When Camden first arrived they'd been riveted to the television. As far as he could tell they had not left their swaying vigil. He ascertained nothing from the snippets of conversation drifting by his ear. It didn't matter. The world for him was completely contained in this dark corner, among the flakes of chicken skin and the greasy piece of paper depicting his life as a snake.

If you were born in one of these years, the text within his pie explained, *you were born in the Year of the Serpent.* Camden thought that was appropriate. He licked from his lips what juice could be sucked off a bone then read on. *You are a clever individual, crafty in matters of bumpy, oh here we go hang on tight family is not as important as with some—*

Camden closed his eyes, opened them, stared at the shadows in the corner. He eventually looked back to the horoscope and tried to read it from the top. The characters swirled within the borders of his pie slice. They grouped into words, broke off, bounced off the lines separating the serpent from the rat.

The booth surged, slid under the wall which folded over him like a wave, then all was still. The wall rose beside him, straight as before. Nevertheless he gripped the edge of the table, and slowly turned his eyes to something rolling towards him in his peripheral vision.

VII.

They ran atop the wave but did not fall. In fact, the vertigo Benjamin felt as they raced along the hospital corridor was more visual then physical. It seemed as if the walls and ceiling bent naturally with the rolling of the floor. The people contained within their writhing confines did likewise. He wanted to be frightened, to scream. His father bled atop the gurney, and the son knew this was no time for such considerations. Benjamin accompanied the EMTs into the operating room. They spouted details to the doctors who ran alongside. No one noticed him. Everyone was busy watching the walls expand and contract.

The dying man's stare pulled Benjamin to him.

"Are we moving?" Adam's voice was stronger, but Benjamin took no solace in the fact.

"Dad, it's OK. We're at the hospital."

"…or is the Universe rearranging itself?"

"What?"

"Excuse me, sir. You need to leave right now." The nurse gripped Benjamin's arm and pulled him backwards. The dying man looked at the ceiling and opened his mouth. The bandages fell loose, too heavy with blood and brain. It was the last Benjamin saw of his father before the funeral.

VIII.

Somewhere deep in the belly of Wong's Diner, employees yelled to each other in Cantonese. After the floor twisted and writhed for a second time, the congregation standing before the television parted, screaming towards their own alcohol-infused havens.

Camden released his grip on the table. The third wave rolled towards the booth, curving the floor tiles, raising the table like a boat in its moorings riding out a storm. Not knowing what else to do, he reached for another piece of chicken. And watched his spoon.

The pinpoint of light, which had appeared moments before in the center of the spoon's belly, was now abnormally bright. It seemed to Camden that the light emanated *from* the soiled metal rather than reflected by it, since no light hung overhead. He considered picking it up, licking the light like a last drop of pudding. He did not.

The light's intensity grew, as did the frequency of the waves. As soon as his invisible corner of the world began falling back into normalcy it would rise again with the preternatural tide. The light from the spoon reached the ceiling, spilled along the cardboard tiles like smoke. Camden watched the tendrils reach along the surface, then whip back and through the ceiling, as if some breach had been attained somewhere far above. This done, the light widened, oscillated dark to light. He looked around. The restaurant was gone.

IX.

The waves lessened in intensity. Benjamin stood in the parking lot, surrounded by abandoned cars and spectators. Together they looked at the starless night above. He thought of how, when lights are dimmed, moviegoers fall silent in expectation. Benjamin sensed that not only here, but across the world the crowd had hushed.

The pavement rippled for a moment then stilled. Benjamin wanted to think about what had happened, if even to plan his father's funeral. He could not. With the silent, chain-smoking crowd around him, he watched the sky and waited for the final chord to strike. All eyes slowly looked to a bright glow spreading quickly across the eastern horizon.

X.

His booth hung in an ocean of black, the depth of which seemed endless. Racing from every direction, a swirling mass of stars coalesced into rivers. These tributaries of light came together under the table, rose as one towards what was once the ceiling. The sky above swam with the tide of a thousand billion stars racing on a predetermined course into the abyss of space.

Camden reached for the geyser before him. Instantly, his physical self merged with the metaphysical river. His arms, legs and head spread atom by atom through this corner of the universe. His soul rose in glorious splendor above the table. Then it stopped. What was once Camden Lee spread along the water-stained ceiling tiles, absorbed into their fiber. He tried to speak, tried to look. But he was broken into basic particles, fused into the panels, physical only in the sense of this new environment.

No sound could reach his mind, no light. Time stretched out, unseen, reaching everywhere at once. Camden wondered if his mind truly existed anymore. He wondered if he was hovering above the booth, a blind, invisible spirit. He wondered if he would ever die.

"No. I'm sorry."

The voice drifted past, settled back atop him. It repeated, over and over. And he could not scream.

XI.

"...Mister Mitchell, I really don't think this is a good time for political double-speak. What the hell happened?"

"Larry, honestly, I haven't got an answer for you. Everything on the planet is the same as it was. But—"

"But everything up there," the host said, pointing up, "is definitely not the same. We deserve to know what happened."

Kenton Mitchell sat lower in the chair and wiped his forehead with a handkerchief. "We're trying to get a bearing on our exact location." He stopped, realizing the line he'd just crossed.

"Our exact location," the host echoed. "Are you saying the Earth moved?"

"We're not saying anything at the moment. We need to—"

"Oh come on. For Christ's sake....excuse me, folks. That sun setting outside our studios is not ours. It's bigger and it's red. We should have been able to see the Big Dipper last night but personally I couldn't find it anywhere. In fact, I couldn't find ANY constellation. Not that there aren't any stars. Oh, no. There's lots of those. I'm no astronomer, Mister Mitchell. But something up there is very, very different."

The other man offered a slow, deliberate sigh. "Listen. The God's-honest truth is we don't know what's going on. We've got theories, the strongest of which is that we passed through some kind of...." He looked down, searching for some rational set of words for the million souls listening. "We think we passed through some kind of hole in space."

A pause, then, "You mean...a black hole. Something like that?"

"Or something. There are any number of possible phenomena. All theoretical, mind you. Perhaps a black hole, or what's commonly known as a worm hole. Something.

"Like I said, until now they've been mostly theory. Whatever it was, we seem to have drifted in, then cast across the universe to where we now orbit a red giant star. The moon appears to be our own, and obviously no man-made satellites were lost, based on the simple fact everyone's watching us on television right now." He knew that by morning he would be out of a job.

"We seem to have come as a package deal."

XII.

Benjamin sat on his father's porch, half-listening to whatever snippets of the CNN interview drifted through the window. The other half of his mind listened to the sounds of men and woman scouring the backyard under a myriad of floodlights, looking for something most knew in their heart would never be found.

"It's kind of strange," the police sergeant said, taking another sip of beer. "Why weren't we all burned up or frozen? It seems kind of odd we materialized the exact distance from that monstrous sun to keep so many things the same."

Benjamin didn't reply. The man sitting beside him arrived at the house after the funeral, and never left. In a way, he was looking for answers just like the scientists and military folk on the grass below, only he sought them through quiet conversation and a beer. Above them, fighting for attention over the spotlights, the stars shone more brilliantly than either man could remember.

As the night progressed, the pinpoints of light rose over the house, then dropped past the trees as the planet rolled on its axis. Benjamin couldn't tell much of a difference in their appearance, but knew that what he looked at, prior to the events of the last two days, had never been seen by human eyes.

The police sergeant shifted in his chair. "Where do you think we are?"

Benjamin kept his gaze on the sky. "There's theory I heard the other day. We never moved. We're at the center of everything, you see. It's just that the universe kind of, well, rearranged itself around us. We didn't change." He raised his beer can skyward. "All of that up there did."

His guest looked at him for a long time, then shrugged. "It's as good as any other I've heard." He sat back. For a while neither spoke, then the sergeant said, "I guess we'll have to come up with a whole new set of constellations now."

Benjamin nodded. He'd already begun looking for patterns, signs to grab onto which would make sense of the universe hanging above him.

About "Y2 Kay"

Let's keep things light for one additional story before I whack you all upside the head with something nasty again.

Look at the title of this next story. I'll give you *one* guess what it's about. Yep, I wrote *and* sold this baby in 1999. The world was trembling in its boots about the pending Year 2000 crisis which never happened. People were buying food and storing it away (you *know* who you are), hucksters were preaching doomsday sermons while selling ten year supplies of dehydrated food to the gullible. And me, I was at my day job, talking with a man named Paul Winslow.

The subject of the Y2K scare came up, and I vehemently denied things were going to be as bad as people thought. Paul asked me, "Then what do you think is going to happen?" At that moment the right side of my brain kicked in and I rattled off a quick summary of what might happen. I was joking, but Paul looked thoughtful and said, "Is that one of your stories?"

I said, "No, but it probably should be, huh?" I wrote the story in a couple of weeks. Sent it off to Seth Lindberg, editor of Gothic.Net, and waited. Once the new year rolled around this story would be as saleable as green meat. But Seth bought it (God bless him). And the world had plenty of forewarning of what was really going to happen on New Years Day, 2000.

Y2 Kay

"...and we're off!" The producer's arm swept down with dramatic elaboration.

The reporter smiled, obviously relieved. "You're a natural, Mrs. Goodman! Is there something you need right now?"

Through her exhaustion, Kathleen Goodman tried to return the smile. "I'm fine, Benjamin. Go run along and do whatever television reporters do during commercials."

The man nodded. "That would be *eat* I believe." Perfect teeth, his Visine eyes never showing fatigue. He walked into the kitchen and pulled a clean coffee mug from the cabinet over the toaster.

Kathleen was tired, more so than she could remember being in a long time. The crew had mounted an oversized digital clock atop the network's television monitor, which in turn sat atop the woman's own large, dark console in the living room. The time glowed a steady red—eleven-thirty-six.

Eleven-thirty-six, she thought. *Lord.*

Any other day Kathleen would be in bed four hours earlier. Wheel of Fortune, a cup of tea then the cold shock of sheets. Tonight was not normal. She sat in her hard-back chair and stared with bemused detachment across the room at the monitor and clock. From the kitchen Benjamin barked orders to the crew and demanded status reports between sips of coffee. The producer, Samantha something, did likewise. Every few moments one of them looked her way, offering a tired but sincere smile. Kathleen wondered if they were secretly afraid the subject of their New Year's Eve special might kick off to the hereafter any minute. She stared at the camera which loomed like a miniature cannon on its tripod in the middle of the room. Maybe their fears were well-founded. Each time that contraption turned its eye her way, she felt as if the peach pit in her chest the doctors called a heart would dry up once and for all.

No. She wouldn't die this night. Too many grandchildren and great grandchildren glued to their sets, waiting for the next installment of "The Woman of Three Centuries." It might distress the family to see their Grandma leaning lifeless in the chair when ABC cut back from Times Square. She wondered if Agnes was watching. Probably not. Her sister would be having the orderlies checking her machinery every fifteen minutes.

Kathleen Goodman was the oldest woman in America, at least the oldest anybody knew about. On August seventeenth she'd managed to crawl forward to her one hundred and eighth year. Everyone wanted to interview this living monument to history—try and understand what it would be like to live in three different centuries. No one *could* know, except a few. In the end, her lawyer grandson Andrew, enjoying early retirement in Boston, helped choose which of the fifty-seven news agencies vying for attention would be her guest tonight. She liked the choice, though felt a little cheated ABC didn't send Dick Clark for the honors.

Benjamin poked his head into the living room. "Everything all right, Mrs. Goodman?"

"Fine," she said. "How long before the next one?"

He looked at his clipboard. "They cut back to us for the final piece at five after twelve.... after the ball drops in New York and the singing and all that yadda-yadda."

Twenty minutes, she thought. *Almost a vacation.*
"I'll just call my sister, then."
He nodded and left the room.

✲　　✲　　✲　　✲

Beep. Whoosh. Beep.

Agnes stared at the darkened television bolted to the opposite wall. As if Death would soon creep out of that gray glass, one second past midnight.

Whoosh. Beep.

"It's going to be OK, Aggie. I promise nothing's going to shut down."

Agnes looked at the nurse. What was her name? It started with a 'B,' didn't it? It wouldn't come. It never did. Not that this deficiency was related to age. Agnes was one hundred years and two months old and could still remember her first day of school. She just had a miserable memory for names.

Whoosh.

The machine continued its cycle unabated, like a mountain river which beyond any reason that comforted her, continued to pour gallons of water year after year. But this wasn't a river, nor any such act of nature. It was a machine, sucking blood from her like a fictional vampire, digesting and spinning the fluid within its bowels, adding nutrients, insulin, regurgitating it back into Agnes' other arm. Unfailing. Relentlessly surging to keep her alive.

Beep. Whoosh.

Ring.

But inside this life-giving monstrosity was a computer. Powerful, untiring, infallible. But a computer. She heard the news reports. What they said about this particular change in year. What was that acronym they kept using? *Y2K. That's it.* Midnight in the new millennium, when all computers with their hard-wired '19's for centuries will change their years from '99' to '00'. The human race will celebrate the year 2000, while the brains embedded in every machine will be thrust back into the Year of our Lord 1900, a time when computers never existed. Not knowing how to handle this new situation, their silicon minds will cease to function. Every elevator will stop between floors. Planes will fall from the sky.

"Aggie? It's for you."

All life support systems and dialysis machines will stop dead. Dead. Like she'll be in fifteen minutes.

"Aggie? Telephone. It's your sister."

Agnes looked at 'B' and tried to smile. The nurse raised the back half of the bed with one hand, held out the phone with the other. Agnes took the receiver with IV-stricken hands.

"Kay? Is that you, Kay?"

"It's me, sweetie. How are you?"

"I'm OK," Agnes lied. "You sound tired."

"You know us television stars," Kathleen's voice said. "Always whooping it up 'til all hours of the night. Did you see any of it?"

"Of course. You looked wonderful."

A pause, then, "You're such a fibber. You haven't turned on a television in forty years."

Agnes felt a giggle well up, but like so many others her big sister managed to create these days, it never evolved past a simple quiver in her stomach. "I suppose not. How come those movie people haven't come here to interview me? This will be my third, well—" but her voice trailed away.

"Oh, Aggie, please stop worrying. You told me the hospital gave you the notice on those machines. Everything's taken care of. The new year's going to come and go and you won't miss a single beep of that infernal contraption you're plugged into!"

"How can you be sure? Everything's so advanced these days. Reader's Digest was talking about micro chips. They said those are the real brains in these things. No one's really sure what kind of stuff is in there, how they'll react. Nothing's like it used to be. No one knows—"

"Yes, they do. For heaven's sake computer brains are more advanced than humans'. Heck, if anything is going to react to the new year it'll probably be—"

"That's just my point!" Agnes interrupted. "How can we possibly have thought of everything?"

"Agnes, please don't get any sicker worrying over something as silly as this. Is someone there with you?"

Agnes looked at 'B' and smiled. "Yes. She's very nice. She promised to stay with me until the end."

Kathleen audibly sighed over the line. "It's not going to end. I promise. I'll call back right after they say goodbye over here. Then I'm going to sleep until Monday."

"Goodbye, Kay."

"I'll talk to you later." Kathleen hung up. Agnes held the phone to her ear a minute longer. When the dial tone kicked in she let it fall to the bed. The nurse hung it up then gently took her hand.

"How's her interview going?"

Agnes didn't answer. The clock on the side table read eleven-fifty-four.

* * * *

Times Square was fuzzy. Kathleen blinked. Her exhaustion was beginning to win the battle. Only three minutes until midnight. On the monitor, the New York crowd bounced like popcorn behind Mr. Clark. In a smaller inset picture, the glowing yellow ball waited with electric impatience for it's descent into history. Benjamin stepped into the room.

"Six minutes until we say goodbye, Mrs. Goodman."

"Fine." Her voice was a whisper. *So tired.* She closed her eyes and dozed off.

* * * *

"Ten!" The shouts began from the nurses' station down the hall. 'B' never took her eyes, or smile, from Agnes.

"Nine!" Beep.

"Eight!" Whoosh.

"Seven!" Beep.

Agnes felt her heart beating in its thin cavity. She tried to pray, to make some final reconciliation before it ended.

"Six!" Whoosh.

"Five!" Beep.

But she couldn't concentrate. The roller coaster was cresting its apex and would never come down again.

"Four!" Whoosh.

"Three!" Beep.

"Two!" It would stay at the top. Whoosh.

Forever.

"One!" The nurse never wavered in her smile, but gently squeezed Agnes' hand. *Such a wonderful young girl.*

"Happy New—"

Beep. Whoosh. A genetically-encoded process, like an internal clock unerringly mapping her lifetime and buried deep within the nurse's mind, rolled over the new year as it had done thirty-six other times since her birth. The nurse's grip loosened. Her eyes rolled up into their sockets. As if in slow motion, she fell back in the chair. Dead weight carried her body to the floor.

Beep.

Whoosh.

Agnes was hungry. She screamed and screamed.

* * * *

Kathleen stared transfixed at the painting across the room. It glowed with the color and brilliance of St. Malachy's stained-glass windows. But the painting was too detailed. Maybe it was a photograph. She'd seen a number of them before. But all that color....

She must still be asleep. The scene before her depicted hundreds of people sleeping on a bright street corner. She concentrated on the image. Maybe they weren't sleeping, after all. Body after body lay atop one another, oddly contorted, an arm now and again twisted the wrong way. *Macabre.* A piece of dust drifted across the scene. Kathleen squinted her eyes to follow its path. It disappeared at the picture's edge. Another appeared. Then another.

Her heart began beating oddly, too fast. Those weren't pieces of dust. Like locusts, swarms of stray confetti and papers drifted across the bizarre landscape of bodies. These things were in the painting, or picture, whatever it was. They moved. The painting was alive!

Kathleen said, "Mom?" Her voice sounded dry, sickly. "Mom?"

At last she pulled her gaze from the image and scanned the room. This wasn't her bedroom. It wasn't even her house. Candles glowed brilliantly from every corner. But the light was wrong, too white, too bright. She gripped the arms of the chair. *Chair?* She'd gone to sleep in her own bed. What was she doing in a strange house sitting in a chair? A mental image of Goldilocks popped into her mind, try as she might to suppress it.

She tried to stand. Every muscle in her body fought the action. She fell back, wheezing.

Oh, God, please. Don't let me be sick.

She thought of that newspaper story her father read, about the epidemic in England. People were dying from influenza faster than the plague of the dark ages. And it was starting to spread here, to America.

No, she thought. *I felt fine when I went to bed.*

Kathleen tried to stand again, and succeeded. Stiff, cold pain spread into her legs and hips.

"Mom? Is anyone here?" Dreaming. Every step, the sound of her voice, all of it felt and sounded like an elaborate nightmare. Her father would be gone until Thursday, selling his brushes. But her mother *must* be here somewhere. It was then she thought of the baby. Something's happened to the baby and they brought Kathleen here while she slept.

Oh, no. Oh, no oh no oh no.

She shuffled towards the kitchen. Why was everything so bright? Then she realized. These weren't candles. The house had electricity! Her fear momentarily fell to the sudden excitement of standing in a house with honest-to-God electric lights. She stumbled over a man's body.

She instinctively threw out her hands to brace the fall. In the instant before she impacted with the floor tiles, Kathleen got the first good look at her skin. Dry, wrinkled, spotted with dark brown blotches. These weren't her hands. They belonged to someone else, an old woman. If they were hers, she was sicker than she feared. When she landed something in her right wrist came loose. Any discomfort prior to this moment faded under the blinding fire in her arm. She closed her eyes and howled against the pain. The grinding in her wrist reverberated even through her teeth.

When Kathleen opened her eyes, a man stared back at her. His gaze was cold, unblinking. Lifeless. In her peripheral vision she sensed other bodies scattered on the floor with her.

This man needed her help. They all did. What in God's name could *she* do? She was only eight years old. Without any reasonable answer, she began to cry. She called for her mother, for anyone, knowing something bad was happening. The disease from England. Everyone was dying. Kathleen closed her eyes and cried through the pain in her wrist, through the image of her shrunken and sickly skin, through the lifeless eyes of the man on the floor beside her.

* * * *

The hospital corridor was silent, but for the steady beeping of the machinery. Slumped in chairs, draped across the half-walls of every workstation, nurses and interns lay as if in drunken slumber. The odor of decomposition overpowered the automatic air fresheners. In one room at the end of one hall, the screaming began again.

The old woman thrashed side to side, oblivious to the panicked beeping of the machine as it compensated for changes in the patient's vital signs. Agnes was hungry. She screamed, her body reverberating with the effort. The two-month-old infant raised its hundred-year-old arms into the air, begging for the breast or bottle which would never come.

About "Ritual"

I came up with the idea for this story a full year before I actually wrote it. I was lying in bed, trying to get my daughter Audrey to go to sleep. I was staring at the swirling patterns of shadow on the ceiling and, like any normal person, saw a goat's head. Like seeing demon shapes in trees (again, like most normal people), once I saw the shape I couldn't see anything else. I imagined the head emerging out from the ceiling, attached to a human body.

Hmm, thought I. Why would it do that? Perhaps a demon (hence the goat's head), or a ghost, or something like that. I had to stop thinking about it because Audrey has a tendency to pick up on my thoughts and gets upset if what I'm thinking involves demons coming out of her ceiling.

Around that time, Steve and Melanie Tem came out with an award-winning novella called *The Man in the Ceiling*, so that kind of squashed my plans for the story. Later, however, I returned to it, deciding that the coming-from-the-ceiling bit wasn't the point of the story, but the visitation itself. And, well, that's why we have dark closets, isn't it?

I honestly don't know why I made the characters Irish. I guess I just liked their names and language, and at the time *Ballykissangel* was a popular television show in the Keohane household.

Ritual

"Would you like to stay up late tonight, Liam?"

"No, Da. It's my bed time."

"Ah, I know. But I just thought, well, seeing—as you're always asking."

The eight year old crawled under the sheets without replying. His father waited for the ritual to begin. Liam squirmed, kicked the sheets, pulled out his arms from the blankets. Slowly settled.

When it came time for Donel's part he paused, not wanting to follow the routine. Not tonight. He wanted his son with him, wanted to ask again, demand, *Liam, stay up late with me.*

Nobody spoke, though the boy normally would be spouting off details about school or a book he was reading. Waiting for the moment his Da was ready to close the door before offering a detailed answer to "what did you do at school today", even if the question had been asked two hours earlier. Tonight Liam remained quiet. He did smile, keeping only to the essence of the routine, quietly, reverently.

Perhaps, Donel thought, the boy didn't understand the significance of tonight. If that was so, wouldn't he have wanted to stay up late? *Liam's coping better than you*, he thought. *He wants to be alone, to sleep away the memory instead of languishing in self-pity like his father.* For one his age the ritual of "bed" overpowered all else, this night more than any.

Donel knelt beside the mattress and tucked the sheet under Liam's chin. Kiss on the forehead. Press of sheets.

Liam turned in the bed's cocoon until he lay on his belly.

Touch of hair. Time for Donel to leave.

"Last chance," he whispered, rising.

"Good night, Da."

Donel began to close the door.

"Da?"

Hope. Donel paused. "Yes?"

"I'm OK. You know?"

The statement was so adult, so certain in tone, his father was mute for a moment. Finally Donel half-smiled and said, "I know." He closed the bedroom door.

* * * *

Tonight was the second anniversary of that bloody moment in his family's life. This seemed now to be an annual ritual. Remembrance. Spending one evening every year before the telly, images flashing by, words buzzing from the speaker, seeing and hearing nothing but the silence of the house.

Donel closed his eyes, head against the back of the couch, and thought about the past. He tried to recapture a moment of happiness, one when Cloida was smiling, crossing the kitchen to embrace him as he arrived home. It never happened, not really. Even before their son was born, his wife existed in a cloud of self-imposed darkness. She emerged often, but then only for a short time. Cloida would inevitably drift back into the tempest of her mind.

Perhaps she saw the road ending from a distance away. Donel sometimes thought so, sitting in this chair, not watching the television. Staring at the wall as if waiting for his wife to step out of the paper's fading pattern, born anew, emerging from the chrysalis where she'd hidden herself.

Every time his train of thought wandered this path, he thought of Father O'Nan. *Where has she gone?* Donel asked once after the funeral. O'Nan's answer of silence sliced a hole in Donel's world, never to be repaired.

She was somewhere lost in her cloud, drifting in the darkness she'd cultivated during her life. That was *not* the priest's unspoken answer, but Donel clung to it. He knew what O'Nan was not saying. Where is Cloida? *Burning for eternity.*

With shaking hand he lifted the glass to his lips and wished Liam had stayed up. Comfort to another brings comfort to oneself, someone had said in the blur of those first few weeks after Cloida's death.

Liam was so small two years ago. His loss was not the same, an absence felt but never understood. Not like Donel's. It's never the same with children. Donel wondered if he might not be slowly brewing his own dark cloud. If so, where would that leave Liam?

* * * *

Liam lay on his side within the sheets. He stared ahead, willed himself still. The bedroom shadows leaned away from the nightlight, casting the room in an angled sleep-time world.

Tonight she would come back, as she had the year before. Da would not understand. His world was work, fixing the car, missing Mum in his own way. Liam wanted to go downstairs and lay on his father's lap, sit beside him on the couch, watch an old movie.

But then he might miss her when she came. Might start to forget. If he was not here, waiting, would she ever come again?

The closet was not in his line of sight, so he did not see something shift in the dark, sheltered from the nightlight across the room by the partially-closed door. The figure moved forward, molding itself from the blackness. Long legged, naked. The figure stepped across the carpet, almost floating. The head of a snake topped the otherwise flawless female body. Its eyes were dark, unmoving. Softly in the light the figure emerged from the closet, drifted toward Liam's bed, keeping out of sight before it stopped, hesitant. It stood like a surreal statue and waited.

Liam stared ahead, forcing his eyes to remain open. Nothing before him. Dark corners bled into the light. His eyes eventually closed in sleep.

* * * *

Downstairs, Donel snapped awake. He'd fallen asleep on the couch again, the ritual broken early this year. Perhaps he was already bored with the repetition. He straightened, lifted his glass and drained the last stale swallow. He checked his watch.

Eleven-fifteen. He still had work tomorrow, get Liam off to school. Donel stood up and went into the downstairs bathroom. He'd check on Liam after, try not to wake him. Let tonight be like any other for his son. Maybe next year it would be so for Liam's father. Cloida went away of her own accord, time to forget and live what life God had in store for the rest of her family.

* * * *

The growing odor, the sense of a presence in the room made Liam's eyes open. Murky vision gritty with interrupted sleep. For a moment he did not remember and gasped when he saw the figure standing before him. Memory returned. He made sure not to look at the face, not to respond.

See me, the figure seemed to say, unmoving, beautiful but soundless. *Acknowledge me. Please....*

Liam stared at the legs, smooth, almost reflecting in the glow of the nightlight. He wanted to look at the figure in its entirety, see it completely. But to do so would be to acknowledge it, and to see the head, which in the periphery of his vision seemed to collapse and expand, shifting first from a snake's then suddenly sprout horns and fur, gray like a goat's, melting again into a muddy lump. He stared at the legs, but knew what was demanded of him—see it for what it was, *who* it was, let the face come into focus, sharply beautiful like he remembered.

He sensed the struggle of the visitor, wanting to reach out to him but unable, a statue of flesh cold to the touch.

Come to me, it didn't say.

Liam slipped from the cocoon of his bed sheet, keeping his eyes downcast, wanting to embrace the perfect legs, let the thing lift him into its trembling arms, hold him and rock him to sleep, sing, coo, shoosh, love.

Remember.

He stared at its feet. The skin around the ankles had dried, lacking its initial luster. It was as if Time itself was blowing like a dry wind about the woman—no, the *thing*.

He risked a look further up until the head was a blur above him. He looked down quickly. Had he seen a dog, angry, snarling, a wolf? Not a goat this time.

I am real....

The corporeal voice was jagged with desperation, tingling through him, trying to pull him forward. Liam struggled to be still. He watched its skin crack, fade to an ashen gray in the glow of the nightlight.

Look at me...I am real.. I am....

It did not say his name, nor had it the year before, or the year before that when Liam awoke loudly from a nightmare. That first night Liam had seen his mother standing by his bed, her head bloody and misshapen. That long ago night the image disappeared quickly, leaving him alone in the room and hearing his father's voice down the hall, *Oh, my God, Cloida, Oh, My God.* Over and over. Not coming into the boy's room for a long time after.

* * * *

Donel ascended the stairs, stopped outside Liam's door. He thought of Cloida, and how it was she who once performed this nightly ritual, walking in and standing beside Liam's bed. She would only stare, waiting to see if he was breathing, drinking in the sight of him before softly walking away and closing the door. She never touched Liam in those moments—fear of waking him. A few moments every night. Donel would stand where he was now, the door ajar, waiting for his wife to emerge glowing in the warmth of a mother loving her son.

On that final night two years ago, she hadn't checked on Liam. She'd gone straight into their bedroom, opened the dresser drawer and pulled out the pistol which she'd kept hidden for God-knew-how-long. When Donel had seen his wife bypass Liam's room he should have known, should have followed her. Instead he waited for his wife to emerge into the hallway with an embarrassed smile. *How could I have forgotten to check on my son?* she might have said.

He'd heard a "pop" and found Cloida in the middle of their bedroom floor, shattered head bleeding into the carpet.

Now, he paused outside his son's room and tried to calm himself. He should have known it was an illusion—getting through tonight without remembering every detail.

* * * *

Forgive me.

The legs rough now, bumpy and gray like wet sand. Liam knew it wasn't too late. He could look up, see the demon before him, say he loved her. He missed her. But a deep part of him, too mature to express, too clear to ignore, knew that such an acknowledgement of its existence, of its *self*, was all it wanted. Forgiveness, remembering who it once was and what it meant to him. He wanted so much to give it to her—to *it*. It was an *it*. But to accept, acknowledge its nature would somehow set it free. He didn't understand completely, but Liam knew if it was free it would never come back.

Something burned, far across distant hills. The odor tickled at the back of his nose.

Legs dried, pillars of cracked brown earth, an ancient monolith, statue of dust and worship for the boy. Then a faded leaf drifted down, skin flaking, falling in autumn.

The right leg shattered. The figure tilted a little before the left leg fell. The body collapsed into a growing pile of itself. Splintering torso falling over knees, breasts indistinguishable from stomach, from the increasingly neglected contents of his sandbox. Smell of burning, shoulders crumbling to dust. Liam followed their descent to the carpet, the pile wide and thick. The face spread out before him, shifting, fading. Liam wanted to stare into its hollowing expression, but closed his eyes instead.

The non-voice screamed, grabbing for whatever lifeline the boy might have been inclined to throw. He hadn't. Eventually the burning smell dissipated and was gone.

Liam lay on his belly, ear to the carpet, and imagined his mother's figure falling back into the place she'd cast herself, a dark world, fire and clouds drifting over statues made of stone and flesh. Everything burning.

It didn't matter. As long as she kept coming back each year to plead with him. Maybe some day he would set her free. He didn't want to forget, nor wanted *her* to forget *him*.

* * * *

Donel opened the door. Liam lay as he had the year before—on his belly in the center of the room, face turned towards the closet door, mouth askew in sleep. He'd fallen off the bed.

Donel walked into the room. The closet door was open. He walked over and clicked it shut, then lifted Liam off the floor and down onto the bed. The sheets were still tight. Donel had to pull hard to make an opening wide enough to gather his son beneath them. He thought about the sheets. Liam couldn't have simply fallen out of bed.

Maybe they'd been sharing the same vigil after all. Though the father would have preferred to share such a moment with the son, he knew everyone had their own way.

Liam did not wake. Donel wondered if he was feigning sleep. He ran a hand across the boy's face, brushing stray hair away. Unlike Cloida, Donel preferred to touch his son each night, feel the reassuring warmth of skin. He'd done it every night for two years, a ritual he relished more than any other. He bent down and kissed Liam's forehead.

Before he closed the door, a small voice said, "Good night, Da."

Donel smiled but did not turn back. "Good night, Liam."

"I won't forget. She was beautiful, you know."

Donel nodded, knowing his son would not see the gesture. "Go to sleep now. You've got school in the morning." He closed the door, and crossed the hall to his own room.

About "White Wave of Mercy"

Fiction writers aren't known for their obsessive research habits. In fact, if we could include a Research Checker on our word processors to accompany Spelling and Grammar, we'd be a lot happier. But sometimes the work at hand calls for some detailed analysis if it's ever going to get off the ground. Brian Hopkins knows this. He's a self-admitted *research junkie* and he edits a series of anthologies in which the stories have to take place in a foreign (but factual) locale. Said locale must be thoroughly understood and/or researched by the author. *Extremes* was very successful, and garnered a Bram Stoker Award nomination. Since then, Brian has edited the Stoker-winning *Extremes 2*, *Extremes 3: Terror on the High Seas*, and *Extremes 4: Darkest Africa*. (*Extremes 5* is in-progress as I write this introduction).

For a while I carried with me an image (which I assumed would one day become a story) of a young boy living on an isolated island somewhere, standing on the beach and seeing the shimmering image of a generic White Man hovering before him. I didn't know what the image would ever develop into, if anything. But stories are like that, sometimes they're not ripe enough to pick yet.

Around the time the call for *Extremes 4: Darkest Africa* came around, there was some media coverage of the AIDS epidemic in Africa. Mostly on National Public Radio, since most other news outlet didn't think that a quarter of the sub-Saharan population being infected with HIV was important enough to cover. In my usual *writerly* way, I began to wonder about Africa, musing conspiracy-like about the motives behind why so many of the Major Powers seemed to be ignoring the issue. Not *completely* ignoring, as there was a growing uneasiness among the world toward a continent with a growing population of orphans. Africa is a large, fertile patch of land, and I began to wonder the old *what if* questions. What if the world powers were simply, well, waiting…?

Anyhow, I wanted to tell this story from the perspective of someone both on the outside of day-to-day events, but at the same time directly affected by them. The Mbuti pygmies are a relatively isolated race of people who live predominantly in the Congo region, also known (sometimes) as Zaire. I read a lot about them (doing my research!!!), and let what I learned guide how my character would react, say or do. I wanted the character Mabeli helpless to do anything about it, though. On a final note, I found a home for the image of the boy on the beach, except the scene shifted into the dark tangled jungles of Africa.

Special thanks to Kevin Duffy, whose wonderful book on the Mbuti pygmies *Children of the Forest: Africa's Mbuti Pygmies* (Waveland Press) was invaluable reading in the development of this story.

WHITE WAVE OF MERCY

'81

The lunchtime crowd at Yvonne's American Deli and Grocery began to wane. The few beleaguered souls too busy to eat at a decent time nodded to the old man as they emerged with bulging take-out bags. Others saw nothing but their next business appointment.

Mabeli sat on the bench and unwrapped his ham sandwich. Olive oil leaked from the corners, but would be absorbed by the paper before ever reaching his slacks. Regardless, Mabeli wore his stains proudly. Everything was too clean these days. In some of the newer buildings in downtown Epulu, the thick humidity and deep green smell of the forest were purified into a dull sameness.

The sandwich was good—one of his vices and a small acceptance of the new world which had emerged around him. Mabeli liked this spot. It was close enough to the edge of the forest that the Ituri rose into view wherever he looked.

"Hi."

"Bonjour!"

The two boys offered reflexive greetings as they hurried inside. Mabeli nodded in return. His French wasn't good enough to try with a mouth-full of ham and bread. The boys—the white one's name was Mike, he thought—were doing what they'd been doing every Tuesday afternoon since school began. Today the new comic books were downloaded.

Was it Tuesday? He'd know if Mike and his friend came out with noses pressed to their readers, lost in adventures that shone from expandable screens.

Mabeli felt the same quick rush each time he saw the white boy, wondering if today was the day. A certainty that they were all being moved, wittingly or not, toward a single event.

So long ago, the memory was clouded by the myriad of experiences in his life vying for attention. Still, Mabeli remembered. Like recognizing a kindred soul on their first meeting, he knew this boy was the one he'd encountered sixty years earlier. Perhaps his hopes had grown too strong to rule out the obvious question. *How* could he be so certain? Time—years—none of that mattered when Mabeli was young. Nor for his people, not then.

Within the relative isolation of the Congo basin, the Mbuti pygmies lived as their ancestors had done for thousands of years. Beyond the protective walls of the forest, the world changed, fell and rose like the tide. It remained, for the most part, *outside* except when the Mbuti ventured beyond the forest to trade, or when an occasional *Muzungu* was drawn into Mabeli's world for research or simple curiosity.

In the end, the *Muzungu* always returned to their own world. Until the day they came in numbers, and never left.

*   *   *   *

'21

Nine-year old Mabeli clambered among the branches in pursuit of imaginary prey. He drove the *mboloko* further through the brush with shouts and the beating of his spear against tree trunks. If the hunt was real, Mabeli would wait by the nets with the other men, letting the women drive the small antelopes their way. In play, however, standing still and waiting couldn't compare to the *chase*.

In one hand, Mabeli carried the small spear he'd made with Akujay's help, when his father was healthy and could sit upright. In his other, a wide mongongo leaf. If someone caught him at play instead of gathering leaves to patch his parents' hut, he could hold it up and say, "See? I *am* gathering them."

But no one bothered him. Yesterday's hunt was short-handed but successful. Enough meat for many meals, including the upcoming festival and more for Kalegi to take into the village to barter. Mabeli would play now. He'd asked his sister to join him, but she remained with their mother at Akujay's bedside.

He knew he should be there as well, display the same concern for his father's illness. Instead he felt anger. For the third time in recent memory, they would soon pack up camp and move on. Mabeli felt a driving need to escape into the woods, alone if not with his sister, and play his games. Chase the *mboloko*.

Too many people were dying. The tribe would have yet another Molimo festival to bring better luck, and dance around the *Kumamolimo*—the festival's central and sacred fire. Pretend it was doing good.

At nine, Mabeli was old enough to understand something evil was among them. The other day a *Muzungu* priest, his once-white skin sun-burnt and peeling, accompanied Kalegi back from the nearby village of Epulu. The priest talked among the tribe, then performed a ceremony over Akujay and others who'd fallen ill.

As he prepared to leave, the priest approached Mabeli. The tall man spoke fluent Kingwana, warning the boy to be careful, speaking of the disease in terms of sexual intercourse, of blood. The ideas had both amused and frightened Mabeli, who quickly excused himself to run to the other side of camp.

Looking back, he regretted the reaction. The priest had stared after him with a look that was akin to fear—for Mabeli and his people. Something very bad had found its way among the pygmy tribes of the Ituri, something which had been ravaging the rest of the continent for a much longer time. Many *Muzungu* had lately tried to explain this, but the concept eluded most as the Mbuti tried to carry on with their lives. How could they accept a disease, especially one revolving so strongly around sex, which even the best roots and herbs could not conquer? It was Death gone out of control.

This afternoon, Mabeli thought none of these things. He saw only his imaginary antelope break free of the bushes. He shouted and hooted, gave pursuit back and forth across the underused pathway. As he rounded a vine-choked mongongo trunk, he saw the spirit.

Mabeli stumbled back and dropped the leaf. The figure was pale, more so than the *Muzungu* priest, almost shimmering in the muted sunlight. The spirit stood no taller than Mabeli's four and a half feet but the face was that of a boy—rounded and smooth. Perhaps he was lost, having wandered too far from the village.

"Who are you," Mabeli shouted, and raised his spear for dramatic effect more than any real malice.

No reply. Instead, the other raised a hand and pointed. Though his lips moved, he had no voice. Mabeli felt a coldness creep into his arms and legs. The reason for the other's odd coloring became apparent. Mabeli could see through him.

A spirit. Perhaps the very *mbolozi* which some suspected of plaguing his people.

"Speak to me," Mabeli said, sterner now. The spirit moved its lips. They stood less than three huts' length from each other, but still Mabeli heard nothing. No voice, no breath. Only the wind through the trees and the constant chatter of wildlife.

His legs twitched. He should leave this place. Sacred or defiled, he did not belong in this creature's presence.

The sprit turned suddenly to reveal a second figure emerging from the air behind it. The first moved its lips again, then blurred and disappeared. The new figure stared, as if in wonder, at Mabeli and spoke with the same silent voice.

The pygmy child felt a scream catch in his throat. He should not show fear. He *would* not.

The second figure was familiar, even in its transparent, wavering state. Its skin was dark with close-cut white hair. When it raised its hand, Mabeli fell to his knees and shouted words that were unintelligible, sounds to reflect his fear. The man in front of him was Akujay, Mabeli's father whom he left wheezing and dying back at camp. He looked much older, but healthy and strong as he leaned on a gnarled staff and regarded the boy.

Mabeli's unwanted tears blurred the forest around him. What should he do? If it was his father, then—

Something moved between them, an animal perhaps, and was gone before Mabeli could see it clearly. He hurriedly wiped away his tears, to find himself alone. The figure had vanished.

Mabeli found his voice. "Father?"

No answer, nor did he expect one. That was not his father. The *mbolozi* was mocking him. Akujay was alive. *He was alive.*

For the first time in his life, Mabeli got lost in the forest in his haste to return home. When he finally found camp he crawled into his parent's small hut. Akujay was there, gasping for breath as he'd been doing all morning.

Mabeli's mother turned to her son and regarded him, keeping one hand protectively on her swollen belly. Her face had become thin, perhaps from tending to her husband, perhaps from the same disease which was stealing away so many Mbuti.

Mabeli looked at his father. The sores on the man's face and arms were either pale white or bruised into indigo. Mabeli had seen none of these on the false spirit. His sister came in and moved to her mother's side. They looked at Mabeli, waiting for him to speak. He said nothing, but backed slowly from the hut.

* * * *

'81

The boys walked past the bench. When they moved on at a good distance, Mabeli rose slowly from the bench and followed. He tried not to look too long in their direction should they turn and see the short old man once again trailing behind them. If they stopped, he would cross the road, perhaps look into a storefront window. The crowd was heavy enough that they hadn't yet noticed him.

The feeling of anticipation in Mabeli's heart quickened as the white boy and his friend crossed at the intersection onto the Rue Ituri, named decades ago by the French-led crew which slowly, methodically, rebuilt the old Congo pass-through (merely an overgrown path during Mabeli's boyhood). It served as the primary thoroughfare to the capitol Kinshasa—the largest city in Zaire. Other roads had been laid out in recent years, smaller tributaries leading Northeast to Niangara and south as far as Kamina and Saint Joseph's.

The sidewalks at this western edge of Epulu were wide, lined with storefronts and vendors. So many people, a mixture of black and white. The term *Muzungu* had long lost its meaning in the mass influx of Americans and Europeans. Some days, Mabeli would spot someone unmistakably African, someone born, like himself, to this land. It had been too long, however, since Mabeli met someone descended from the pygmy tribes. Most that survived the plague still lived in the reservations outside of Likasi. But their numbers dwindled as the New World slowly closed around the basin.

The boys stopped on a vacant bench to return to their comics. Mabeli passed by, careful not to look in their direction.

If this was the day, the boys would eventually follow.

Here at the boundary of the city, the edge of the Ituri forest rose high. Mabeli watched road crews clear away branches and pull shoots from the ever-present cracks in the road. These men were state-compensated ants, keeping the Congo at bay while the rising presence of the city slowly pushed of its own accord.

Mabeli followed the curve of the Rue Ituri and entered the shaded twilight of the forest. Here under the canopy, the sidewalk remained wide enough to accommodate bicycles and pedestrians, before narrowing to a more respectable (and maintainable) level. Mabeli let the cool green light move over him. As always, the sensation of entering his real home returned with such power. He breathed the overpowering aroma of life, and searched out a new bench upon which to rest, and wait.

✳   ✳   ✳   ✳

'35

"Are you the leader here?" The speaker was a tall white man with a short-clipped moustache.

Mabeli waited for the translation from a second man, an Angolan dressed in much the same manner as the first—a uniform donned by so many, lately. The Angolan soldier translated the question from French into rough Kingwana. Mabeli stiffened, more at the original tone with which the question was asked than the words. The first man's face was tight, not from rage as much as defense, a self-enforced mask against the presence of so much death around him.

Someone guided Mabeli's sister off his arm. She was too tired to stand and wait for her brother to deal with these men, and needed to cope with her own grief. It didn't matter how much the strangers' arrival, and medicine, had been a blessing. Kalegi had been her husband and she had the right to ignore the visitors for the moment. Mabeli let her go reluctantly, and gave his full attention to the tall Frenchman.

"We have no leader," he said quietly. "We do not believe in governing by only a few."

The Angolan translated. Mabeli still had trouble understanding the *Muzungu's* varied languages. Kalegi once explained that some spoke a language called French. The other was the more guttural, syllabic tongue of English. Mabeli understood little of either, but enjoyed the cadence of the French.

The white man looked puzzled. The Angolan spoke further in French, perhaps explaining Mabeli's answer. Finally, the first asked, "Then who can I talk to?"

Mabeli shrugged at the translation. "You can speak to me."

After Akujay, Mabeli's father, passed away the tribe did as they had always done and abandoned camp for a new part of the forest. No matter where they went, how many seasons passed or Molimo festivals danced, the disease slowly, methodically, ate away at the age-old barrier between Mbuti tribes. As their numbers decreased, they eventually came together out of reluctant necessity. Daily life improved for a while, but the plague did not end.

The final wave of newcomers found them. Most were physicians and laborers, or an occasional priest (Mabeli never again saw the priest he'd met as a boy). Soldiers for protection should their presence not be welcomed. The people brought medicine. Most came from countries whose names Mabeli could never quite pronounce, or from the northern regions of Africa. They called themselves the United Nations. Mabeli thought it an admirable term.

They arrived to help. A white wave of mercy descending upon the Congo with open hearts and promises of aid for a stricken people. The medicine *did* help, but it did not cure.

"Too expensive," said a physician from a recent group. "Too many of you have been infected." The impact of her words, spoken with an honest sorrow, fell greatly upon Mabeli's heart. Until that moment, he assumed there was no cure for the plague—no hope that the physicians could stop its onslaught.

There *was* a cure, of some kind, in some form. But it was not for them. *Too many infected*, she had said.

Mabeli thought of his mother struggling for breath only a few seasons after his father died. He thought of his baby brother born that year, emerging from the womb already sick, living no longer than his first few weeks. Even Kalegi could bring nothing useful back from the Epulu village except news of more sickness and death. Now his widow, Mabeli's sister, moved through the days with liquid lungs.

Too many. Surely, he thought, they could have saved one of them.

The large Frenchman looked at the pygmy for a long time, his stern mask slipping into a hesitancy which worried Mabeli. "We have to ask," he said, "that you and your people relocate, so we can better help."

The Angolan translated, then looked back at the Frenchman with a hard stare that offered Mabeli some hope, some unspoken alliance.

Mabeli could have objected, but what would it accomplish? Only four adults in the tribe, not counting the seven elders who found their increasing responsibilities more daunting every day and a few children finally reaching a rebellious maturity.

He looked at both soldiers, nodded once, and walked away.

The village of Epulu seemed to have tripled in size since Mabeli's last trip to barter. His people arrived with their UN escorts and were led onto a waiting truck. Mabeli stayed behind. His sister wailed and tried to drag him up to sit beside her. He touched his sister's cheek, careful to avoid the sores which had formed there.

"I need to stay," he said. "Here—in the village for a while. I have to understand what's going to happen. To see."

She stared at him so intently Mabeli wondered if perhaps she could read his thoughts. *Please understand. I cannot watch you die, too.* "I'll join you soon," he said. "I promise."

The truck pulled away. Only then did Mabeli realize he still held his sister's walking staff. An acacia branch, trimmed and polished for her by an elder. Mabeli instinctively moved to abandon it against the side of a nearby building, then stopped to examine it more closely. The limb was gnarled and thick, quite sturdy. Standing in the settling dust of the truck carrying away his tribe, Mabeli found within it a reassuring familiarity. He would keep it, for a time at least.

When the French soldier saw Mabeli he tried to usher him towards the next caravan.

"This is my home," the pygmy replied. "I'm not sick, as you can well see. Unless your intentions for my people are other than you have mentioned, I'll go now and find a place to stay." The Angolan soldier gave the translation then laid a firm hand on the Frenchman's arm. Mabeli walked into the village.

Talking with those villagers who spoke his tongue, he learned what their world had fallen into. Then he could listen no further. Mabeli stayed in his cramped room within the burgeoning UN compound for three days without emerging.

Three-quarters of the sub-Saharan African population was gone. Dead, or soon to be. Mostly adults, leaving as their survivors children with no one to lead them save the very old, who in turn had none to care for *them* but the children.

The feared instability of such a population, one crumbling national government beside another, finally pulled the United Nations to its occupation. The world moved in to save and control a devastated continent. A wave of mercy, or an invasion. To Mabeli, when he finally stepped from his room, it made no difference.

If the newcomers chose to save some of his people, even at the expense of taking their land, then perhaps there was hope. The decision, it seemed, was not his to make.

* * * *

'81

Mabeli's heart skipped a beat as the two boys came down the path. *This is the day*, he thought again. The crawling of his skin as they approached, the electric smell in the air, the increasing clarity of that long-ago memory, all told Mabeli it was true.

From the moment of that brief vision in his childhood, Mabeli felt a thread connecting him to something *beyond* himself. As his life in Epulu wound out, Mabeli found himself with too much time to think, to remember. He held no job, save the occasional employment taken more for distraction than obtaining means. The reparative social programs enacted for the Mbuti and other displaced natives adequately carried him along day to day, year to year. The memory cultivated in his mind and settled among the mundane events in his life, and the meaning of what he'd seen slowly dawned. He'd made a mistake in those earlier years trying to define it.

What he saw was not his father nor some *mbolozi* from another realm, but a glimpse into a future that did not yet exist. He saw himself. A thread, unraveled between two moments of the same soul. This thought, and hope, Mabeli held close as the world he knew collapsed around him, only to rise from its ashes as something *other* than his home. Buildings challenged the jungle before them and Mabeli found himself adrift in a sea of foreigners flocking to their "new world". As he shuffled along well-paved streets into old age, the chance of reconnecting with his past, if only for a moment, became a lifeline.

He knew what would happen as he leaned on his walking stick and rose from the bench, once again following the boys. He did so with a clarity of purpose, as in a dream, and dared not question it without the risk of missing his destination. The end of the thread.

The sidewalk began to narrow where the white boy named Mike stopped. His friend walked on a moment longer before turning and calling back. Mabeli was close enough that he should hear, but the sounds of the forest and occasional traffic were drowned by a buzzing inside his own head.

Expectation. Maybe terror. The sound of blood pulsing through his temples.

Mike stared at something just inside the tree line. The friend, a few paces ahead, stood on tip-toe to see what Mike saw. He asked, "Qu'est-ce que c'est?"

Mabeli was almost upon them.

"It's OK," said Mike in English, not to his friend but to some unseen third party. Mabeli reached the boy and stopped, perhaps too close. Mike wheeled around in surprise.

"Hey," he said. "What are you doing?"

Mabeli ignored the question and moved in front of him. Mike lashed out half-heartedly then muttered something under his breath about "that crazy old man from the store". He joined his friend down the sidewalk. They stopped a safe distance away and watched with nervous curiosity.

Mabeli raised a shaking hand to his mouth and looked at the image of himself standing just inside the trees. The young boy, naked save for a single strip of cloth covering his genitals, stooped lower, a small spear raised defiantly. His ash-black skin shimmered. The old man noted without surprise that he could see the blurred outlines of the foliage behind him.

He thought, *What do I say?* then whispered, "Everything is fine," in the old Kingwana tongue. The boy would understand nothing else. "Do you know who I am?"

The boy spoke, shouting, but no sound came forth. With an expression of slowly-dawning terror, young Mabeli dropped his spear and sank to his knees. He shouted again, and the old man knew the boy was screaming. Mabeli felt time slipping away, the thread thinning. His heart beat with renewed urgency. So many years leading to this moment. He had to concentrate, come up with the right words, knowing they would never be heard. "Mabeli," he said, "understand this, there are some—"

A bicycle whizzed along the path between them. Mabeli gasped in surprise and stepped back. Two more followed the first, one ridden by a young white woman in a tight riding suit, long blonde hair trailing behind. The other two were dark and equally as lean. They curved around the corner and were gone, the hissing of their tires fading towards the city. The two boys snickered from their safe vantage.

The old man squinted into the foliage. Young Mabeli was gone.

Mabeli felt the cold emptiness of this loss deep in his chest. He stepped through the mongongo leaves and stood in that spot of so many years before. Mosquitoes swarmed about his face. He ignored them.

The ground was damp in the shadows. Mabeli kicked a piece of trash under a fallen leaf. The air was green and lush. For a moment, he imagined himself back home among these trees, flushing out imaginary antelope, chasing them into the nets and trying not to think about his father.

He thought of Akujay now, what details he could recall, of his mother and sister, and Kalegi. All gone. Maybe they were here again. From where Mabeli stood, all was as it used to be, green and brown under the mid-afternoon sun. The Ituri in its splendor. He heard a car race past along the jungle road, heading east towards Kinshasa. Mabeli imagined the two boys were still there, waiting for the crazy old man from the store to emerge back onto the sidewalk.

If he stepped forward, however, perhaps he could follow what was left of the thread back to the lost people of his childhood. In any case, Mabeli knew, he would be returning home. He leaned on his staff and began to walk, letting branches slap against him and fall away. The forest blurred at the edges of his vision, like it had done that fateful day so long ago. Mabeli saw it as a good sign. He continued on, deeper into the forest, leaving the world of the *Muzungu* further behind.

About "Bark"

The next story is another original story for this collection. I affectionately refer to this one as *Incineration in the Woods*. Dares-gone-awry are such great fodder for horror stories. Maybe some day I'll write more and make a new collection called *Dares are Bad!*

"Bark" is probably the most graphic of any of my stories, and originally that was my intention. You may not believe it after reading this, but by the time I finished with the version of "Bark" that follows, I'd toned it down quite a lot. I also have a version that takes place during the daylight. Long story. There is a vague but deliberate secondary theme in this one which I won't explain, except to say that the names (both normal and unique) I chose for the characters were very intentional. If you figure it out, let me know.

There's not a whole lot else to say about this one, except maybe *Dares are Bad*.

Bark

The rumors surrounding Bark were almost as big as the dog itself. Someone's arm reportedly severed at the bicep. Human bones scattered across the doghouse floor.

The Newfoundland's world was an oversized paddock, thirty feet by thirty feet, set back from the old woman's nineteenth century Victorian. The surrounding chain link fence rattled in the wind that tore up the mountainside. Electric blood flowed through its veins, pumped from the small transformer half-hidden among the trees.

For the past five days the house had, by all signs, remained vacant since the old woman's death. It stood as a looming shadow silhouetting the starlight. The yard was silent. The uncut Spring grass bent under its own weight. The woman had family, somewhere, who had been called in when she fell ill. Any attention to her property by the heirs was minimal.

At least Bark was not laying dead in his paddock, though the ground within reeked of feces. The doghouse, like its human counterpart, was a dark shadow in the middle of the pen. And it was big.

Tonight, three figures shifted among the tree shadows bordering Bark's paddock, spirits bathed in the quicksilver light of the waxing moon. They knew they were alone on the property. There would be no witnesses.

David sat on the ground and slipped off sneakers and socks. Climbing the fence with any form of insulation was deemed "unfair."

He took Robin Fae's dour expression as concern. An illusion, David knew. Most likely she was worried he'd survive her dare and collect his reward. Which, of course, he would. He'd done his research.

Bark was in the dog house, asleep—or whatever coma monster dogs fell into at night. It *was* there. He heard it breathing from somewhere inside its lair. David pulled off the final sock, stood and smiled. It was a quiet, mischievous grin.

A few feet away, the fence hummed in expectation.

*   *   *   *

Robin Fae tried not to admire how good the bastard looked, and was grateful for the darkness. It masked any look of appreciation she might let slip. Early May and the guy sported nothing but a pair of jeans and white tee-shirt. New Hampshire blood ran thick. He didn't even seem to mind the constant barrage of mosquitoes and May flies hovering around him. For her part, Robin wore an oversized LA Raiders jacket. One of the few reminders of what used to be "home" before her clan moved to North Conway a month ago. She'd be shivering until mid-summer at this rate.

The bulky jacket served another purpose—to keep herself as shapeless as possible. Not that it mattered tonight. All this guy had to do was scale the fence, touch ground, and clamber back over without being eaten. If he did that, he'd see plenty.

As if reading her thoughts, David smiled. "Don't worry," he said. "I'll let you keep your socks on when I collect the bet."

"You'd be done before I had time to take them off," she whispered. "Besides, even *if* you don't get your dick bit off by Bark, we're not doing it here."

David's shadowed face darkened further, reminding Robin why the bet might have been a mistake.

Caveman takes prize. Caveman keeps prize.

She hoped his dick *did* get bitten off.

David's buddy Quince hunkered down and gripped a handful of tree roots. He was always grabbing something, as if without an anchor his excess energy would toss him away in the wind.

"OK, people," Quince whispered. "It's show time. Davey, give me five to work around the other side. When you hear me, move your ass. I'm cute, but I might not be little Barky's type." With that, he scurried through the trees, soundless, a mythical *Puck* looking for mischief in the White Mountains. He kept his flashlight low to the ground, raising it only when he stumbled into a bush or tree.

Left alone, neither of them spoke again. David knew there'd be time to get cozy later. After he did what he had to do, and if—*when*—Quince did his part.

Come on, dude, he thought. *Keep your head straight* one *time.*

He hoped the girl didn't notice sweat trickling down his armpit. Not because of the fence. It was the dog that worried him. He closed his eyes and pictured Robin's elusive body wriggling beneath him. It helped keep things in perspective. Of course, he wasn't the only member of the senior class who craved a look under those impenetrable layers of clothing, vying for a peek when she passed in the hall.

Last month, when she first walked into English Lit during yet another mind-numbing discussion of Billy Shakespeare, David found his attention wandering from its usual fixation out the window. He'd stare at the exposed nape of her neck as she followed along with the lesson, catch the faint outlines of her shoulder blade, the strap of a bra. She never looked back, and this inaction spoke volumes to him. She'd known he was staring, girls *always* knew. The Bitch enjoyed the attention, and had come up with this ludicrous dare as an excuse, a chance to say "I didn't give in, it was just a bet." He knew the truth. She wanted to know what David Lysander had under *his* clothes as much as he wanted to learn what lay under hers.

* * * *

Quince screamed. He fell to his knees, threw his head back and howled. The sound trickled to a slow, demented laugh. He stood up and looked inside the fence, squinting as if the act would lessen the gloom beyond. Nothing.

"Yoo-hoo. Mister Doggie—wake up!" Quince grabbed the chain link fence and rattled it. He stopped when he realized there was no shock, not a speck of electricity coursing through him. *What the—*. He remembered the Bitch's bizarre rule and kicked off his Nikes. He tried again.

A million invisible mice ran up his arms and tried to pry open his skull. Quince jumped back, waited for the spots floating in front of him to fade. The tingling in his arms slowly subsided as his eyes traced the thin feed wires interlaced with the links.

Davey's going to climb that? he thought. There was too much juice—

Something big emerged from the dog house. Black fur glistened in the moonlight. Its head turned right. Davey and Robin were still out of sight, Quince hoped. The black thing sniffed, and the yard filled with a low rumbling growl. It looked to its left.

For a brief moment Quince and the dog stared at each other across the shit-cluttered paddock.

Then Bark exploded towards the fence. In the pale light its hind quarters looked too thin compared to the oversized head and chest, as if the creature was constructed of two halves of entirely different breeds of dog. But its disproportionate bulk belied its speed. Heavy paws padded on the dirt. Quince shouted as Bark slammed into the fence. The dog yelped and fell back.

Then, BARK! BARK! BARK!.

"Christ," Quince said. "Shut the fuck up, man!" It was a startled reaction on his part. No one would hear.

BARK! BARK!

Davey emerged from the shadows and was now walking quickly towards his side of the fence. Quince forced himself to stare only at the dog. He couldn't warn them about the fence without blowing the whole deal.

BARK! BARK!

They'd never hear him over the damned dog, anyway.

Bark stepped forward, remembered the fence. It paced sideways. Quince wondered if the dog had been fed since the old woman kicked off. The thought sent a small wave of pity, and dread, through him.

BARK!

At the fence, Davey didn't reach for it as much as leap upon it like a crazed animal.

Quince shouted to mask the sound of his friend hitting the fence. He shook his head, stuck his tongue out and blew a raspberry. He stared the dog in the eyes. Big wet eyes reflecting meager light around it. Quince's own shouts and meaningless taunts were drowned in a sea of BARK! BARK! BARK!

*   *   *   *

When David heard Quince he smiled and thought, *What an idiot.* He waited until Bark seemed appropriately preoccupied then walked forward.

He had to be careful where he hit the fence. Most important was to avoid the three copper wires running along the bottom, middle and top. The darkness wasn't going to help him much with this. As soon as he was in the air, he would no longer be grounded and therefore safe. Apparently Robin had forgotten about birds sitting on power lines, even *if* the makers of the fence hadn't. The copper leads were ground wires. If he hit one, the circuit would be complete—his body the breaker.

He leaped forward and hit the fence as quietly as possible. Nothing. Not even a buzz in his ears. For the girl's sake, he took in a sharp intake of breath, released one hand from the links as if about to fall back onto the ground.

Feigning a massive internal struggle he reached up, as close to the top as possible without hitting either the ground wire or pole running along the top of the fence. Like its counterparts stuck into the ground every eight feet, the top pole was a primary grounding rod. *The third rail*, David thought. Getting over it would require a sizable leap. No way Bark wasn't going to hear *that*. Still, he'd be back over before the mutt could even turn around. David wondered what Quince must be thinking, since he hadn't let him in on the deception. His friend never had a very good poker face.

*　　*　　*　　*

"Yaaaa, sucker!!! Bite this!" Quince thrust his pelvis forward and Bark slammed into the fence again. A pained yelp, followed by BARK! BARK! BARK! BARK!

The boy danced in a tight circle, careful to prevent the dog from moving too much left or right, risk it seeing Davey who was nearly at the top of the fence already. He tried to ignore the tiny voice relegated to the back of his mind, *Bark probably hasn't eaten in almost a week.*

"Boody boody boody," he whispered, puckering his lips for a kiss. Bark wanted *so* much to chew his head off. Easy to read a dog like that, he thought.

BARK! BARK! BARK!

"Bark! Bark! Bark!" Quince echoed. He wondered why the old lady hadn't snuffed this monster a long time ago and gotten a Pekinese like other people her age.

BARK! BARK! BARK! BARK!

"Bite Me!"

* * * *

Robin knew what the fence was like. She'd tested it herself to gauge what David would have to endure. She'd been able to hold her finger to the links no longer than a couple of seconds.

A barrier that potent shouldn't be legal. Still, knowing the jerk wouldn't get more than an inch or two off the ground gave her courage to suggest the bet. If nothing else, it might stop his incessant staring in class, turn his gaze down a few notches. She'd insisted the dare be carried out tonight, before either of the boys had a chance to check out the juice for themselves.

Watching David reach the upper links, she was certain no normal person could have lasted this long. Meanwhile, his retarded friend kept distracting Bark with his own unbridled hysteria. Robin Fae no longer felt the scales tipping her way, watching this boy—willing to fry his brain for a quick tumble. She surprised herself by becoming more aroused the higher he climbed. Just before everything went to hell, Robin wondered if maybe New Hampshire wasn't such a bad place to live after all.

* * * *

OK. Have to make this quick. David sagged down on his weight, preparing both to pull himself up and over in a single heaving swing, and to add to the dramatic play we was undertaking. It needed to look as if he was about to fall, unable to take any more pain. *Yea, right. Keep wishing, bitch.* He sagged further, then tightened his muscles and pulled upward.

He didn't make it. David landed flat-bellied on the pole and draped over the top of the fence.

* * * *

Quince saw his friend reach the top. He'd done it—climbed what amounted to a small mountain of electricity. Robin *had* to be fucking impressed. At the moment, however, Davey seemed to be stuck at the top.

BARK! BARK!

"Yea, yea!"

Bark paced side to side, never taking his eyes from him. *Good doggie*, Quince thought. *Just keep looking at me.*

In a pang of envy and still shoeless, Quince reached with his right hand and curled two fingers around a link. It must have been his overactive imagination the last time. Electricity coursed though his arm, hitting his brain, squeezing his eyes.

Still he tried to hold on.

As in a dream he saw Bark lunge, the flash of teeth, no yelp this time but a quick retreat. When the world came back into focus, Quince was sitting on the ground, crumpled and dazed.

The dog had just pushed him off the fence.

"What the hell did you—"

The pointer and middle fingers of his right hand were gone past the second knuckle. They erupted like a volcano, spewing inky blood down his arm, onto his leg, dripping to the ground. All he could do was whimper, then scream.

* * * *

Every nerve, every pore in David's body begged him to let go and fall back. But hanging midway over the fence, he didn't know which way "back" was. A numbing blanket spread along his belly, up his arms and legs, into his head. It sucked his balls into his throat.

Let go, his brain screamed. *Fall. Do SOMETHING.*

The dog's paddock blurred below him, melted into the screaming form of Quince beyond. The scene fuzzed into a spotty mesh of colors which bled away to grainy black and white. David wondered if his eyes were melting.

Something sizzled in his ears. He tried to throw himself off, but his body had fallen asleep. All he could do was rock himself back and forth. At least he *thought* that was what he was doing. The world turned upside down. Through the blackness filling the corners of his vision, David watched the ground slam into his face.

The unrelenting assault on his senses cut out. Bright spots lingered around him like moths. David's numb legs bent over him, dragging him sideways. His face twisted against the dirt and the world kept spinning. The moths scattered. He saw ground, fence, trees, finally sky.

Everything stopped. Bright, bright stars overhead.

* * * *

Bark chewed on the bones and gristle from Quince's fingers, then licked blood from its muzzle.

Thump.

The dog turned, saw David lying within the fence. Normally, caution would tug at its instincts, forcing the dog into a slow circle as it growled in warning.

The blood in its mouth sang, *More there. More there.*

Bark swallowed and trotted towards its meal.

* * * *

David couldn't move or turn his head. He saw nothing more than the million pinpricks of light above him and heard only the rustling of the budding trees outside his vision. Then he felt it, the rhythmic *thump, thump* of Bark's heavy paws running his way.

* * * *

Robin watched the dog running for the fallen boy and waved her arms.

"Get away! No, Bark, bad Dog!" She slammed against the fence. If she was hit with electricity she didn't feel it.

Bark stopped a moment over David's body, tilted its head sideways to consider whether the girl was worth its attention. She wasn't. The dog sniffed David's leg and took a tentative step backwards. The boy didn't move. A slower approach, more sniffing.

Robin shouted, "Someone help us, please." *Stupid*, she thought. If nobody had heard Quince they wouldn't hear her.

Bark stopped sniffing and bit David's calf. Just an experiment. A bite and another quick back-step. No reaction. The dog wagged its tail and bit down a second time.

* * * *

David slowly regained feeling in his body, but for some reason couldn't move. The first bite was a simple pressure on his calf. The second sent thin glassy spikes up his leg. Tugging, more pressure, this time higher up his leg. His thigh.

Not down there. Not down there. Please.

David could only see a large black bulk moving below his line of vision. The new pressure on his leg let up suddenly, then returned. Heavy, metallic shards of pain. He tried to determine which part of his body—

No, no, no.

Bark clamped down on David's crotch and shook its head from side to side.

* * * *

Robin shoved a broken branch through the fence. Bark skittered sideways, just out of reach.

Across the way Robin thought she saw Quince stumbling away backwards. The boy was mad with panic, holding his arm and howling unintelligibly. *Oh Christ*, she thought. *Now what?*

She looked around, registering only that the dog was backing away, David in tow by his balls. She ruled out the possibility of climbing the fence.

Across the yard Quince disappeared behind a small outbuilding.

Robin ran into the woods. The boy who was being eaten alive within the fence screamed, but she never looked back.

This isn't my fault, she thought.

* * * *

Bark held fast and dragged David towards the doghouse. Its senses were overpowered by the gushing taste of blood. It shook a mouthful of flesh and denim loose, then paused a moment to chew.

* * * *

When David tried to scream again, something caught in his throat. His arms flopped uselessly at his sides. He understood what the dog had just done, from the sudden emptiness in his gut. An overwhelming physical sensation of loss, like losing a tooth magnified a thousand times.

No pain, not even the glass spikes of earlier. His body had fallen numb below the waist. He wondered if he'd broken his back in the fall.

David swallowed hard, managed to scream, "Help me," but the words came out as gurgles. He coughed, flexed his fingers. They worked better now.

He might have a chance.

Bark dug its teeth into David's other thigh. The numbness blew away. Pain burned through his body, into his skull. The air around him crinkled, then collapsed into blackness. He tried to yell, to fight the onset of this new, terrible darkness.

The ground raked his skull as he was dragged towards the doghouse. He tried to kick with his free leg. Something went loose in his gut. The blackness around him solidified. New shards of glass in his belly, tearing into him.

Someone help me.

*   *   *   *

Quince held his wounded right hand against his chest and staggered into what he prayed was a tool shed. The bleeding hadn't abated, but he'd glimpsed what the dog was doing to Davey and knew there wasn't any time. He'd find a way to stop his own bleeding later.

He pulled the small flashlight from his pocket and looked for…what? A weapon, he decided, maybe something to climb the fence with. He tossed a shovel aside with the tip of the flashlight, considered the garden shears only for a moment. A splinter from the old floor dug into the bottom of his foot.

Outside David screamed one long, horrible wail.

A pick-ax, the curved blade narrowing to a point on one side and flattened like a hoe on the other, leaned against a pair of moldy fence posts. The fiberglass handle was bright orange. Quince didn't know whether fiberglass was safe against electricity, but when he pocketed the flashlight and grabbed it the head was reassuringly heavy. He carried it with his good hand and stumbled outside.

Glass broke nearby. Quince wondered if it was his mind shattering.

He saw the dog's rump collide with the corner of the doghouse. Quince stared at Davey to see if he was moving. His friend's white tee-shirt was dark, blood-splattered. Bark buried its muzzle against the boy's belly, then the scene blurred away. All Quince saw was the fence.

Ten feet to his left was the padlocked gate. He ran to it and hefted the pick over his head, using his damaged right hand only as leverage. He swung the pointed end downward.

It slid through a link, just shy of the lock. Quince fell forward, managed to stop himself before hitting the fence. When he pulled the pick free no bolt of electricity ran through the handle.

Small victories, he thought.

His fingers throbbed. His blood made orange handle slick. He'd have one more shot. Again, Quince raised the pick, focused on the lock, saw where he needed to hit then swung down hard.

The shackle snapped into two pieces, one half falling away with the lock's case. The pointed end of the pick buried itself in the ground an inch shy of his foot.

The gate swung open. Quince pulled his makeshift weapon from the dirt and noticed a metal bar stretched across the bottom of the entrance. He carefully stepped over it into Bark's world. He was greeted by another low rumbling of thunder. At some point while Quince was smashing at the gate, Bark had raised its head from Davey's belly and watched him. It bared red-stained teeth, the black fur around its mouth glistening in the moonlight.

It's too late! He's dead! Turn around. It's too late.

*   *   *   *

While Quince was fumbling through the tool shed, Robin Fae clambered onto the back porch of the Victorian and pulled a key from her pocket. She unlocked the glass door and slid it open. David's sudden scream crawled up her back, but she could not stop.

They'll say it was you. The temptation to simply leave and let nature run its course followed her across the kitchen. She couldn't consider that, couldn't stop moving else the thought might take too strong a hold. She lifted the phone and dialed 911. Almost immediately a voice on the other end said, "North Conway Police Department, this call is being recorded..."

"The dog's gone crazy!" she shouted, holding the phone away as if the glow of the number pad might reveal her face to the man on the other end. "We need an ambulance!"

She dropped the phone to the floor, hoping this hick town could trace the call as easily as a *real* city. A voice buzzed from the receiver, but Robin was already back outside, closing the slider, locking it and pocketing the key. She hesitated. The key. Only she and her father had one. The phone's number pad glowed mockingly across the kitchen. She lifted an old dented milk box, long unused and half-filled with rain water, and tossed it through the glass slider.

Then she ran, hoping no one would realize the mysterious intruder had broken into her grandmother's house only *after* calling the police.

She turned around, saw Quince stepping into the open gate. The dog could now escape any time it wanted. "Oh my God," she whispered. She ran, welcoming the shadows, the cover, the embrace of the trees all around her. All the while, one thought played over in her head. *You should have fed Bark. You should have fed Bark....*

* * * *

Bark approached slowly at first, but the dog's hesitation couldn't compete with the blood-lust and it began to run.

Bark was fifteen feet away. Quince hadn't thought of what to do next. He screamed and ran towards it, stopping suddenly to swing the pick ahead of him. It missed. Bark skittered to a stop.

Quince spun completely around with the momentum of the swing. The dog leaped forward. Quince kept turning, bringing the pick hard against Bark's head. The dog yelped and staggered away. The blade had connected sideways. He hadn't hit it right. At the most, Quince figured Bark had a cracked skull.

The gate was directly behind him. All he had to do was turn and run, somehow get the gate closed.

Davey's leg twitched, as if pleading with him to stay.

In one motion Bark stopped shaking its head and charged. Quince wasn't ready. Two hundred pounds of black dog fell on top of him. He landed on his back and kicked at its belly.

BARK! BARK! BARK! in his face, the smell of hamburger and blood.

Bark opened its mouth and bit down. Quince slammed the pick's handle between the teeth, all the while kicking and squirming. Claws from one paw ripped into his right side. He screamed. Bark backed away one step, pulling at the handle.

At last, one of Quince's feet connected with a soft spot in the dog's underbelly. Bark howled in pain and the pick came free. Quince lifted it over his head, repositioning his grip. One end of the blade hit the ground behind him—he prayed it was the flat end. Bark lunged for his throat.

Quince bent his legs under the dog for leverage and swung the weapon overhead. The point slammed into the top of Bark's skull. The dog's teeth scraped along his neck, but the jaws never closed. Quince kicked at its belly again as a bucketful of blood poured off the dog's head into his face.

He stopped kicking. Bark's tongue slid from its muzzle, fell wetly against Quince's Adam's apple.

It was a long while before he dared move. Then, carefully, the boy wriggled out from beneath the dead weight of the animal and turned his head. He spat out a mouthful of dog blood then knelt on the ground, vomiting in massive, wracking heaves. When he finished, the taste of Bark's blood still lingered.

He pulled off his wet shirt, wiped his face. His right side had three shallow gashes, but the bleeding from the lost fingers had slowed to a trickle. He didn't think that was a good sign.

Quince got to his feet and ran, fell, stumbled across the paddock. He couldn't look for very long. Davey was ripped apart. Between the torn legs, his crotch was a hole with an exposed curve of tubing. The skin over his stomach had been peeled back like a grape's.

Quince sagged into a sitting position against the doghouse. Every time Quince wondered numbly if his friend was dead or not, Davey's chest moved up and down, accompanied by bubbly wheezing. He considered going for the boy's chewed-but-still-intact belt, wrap it around his own arm to stem what flow remained from his fingers. The idea of touching Davey anywhere made him look away.

In the entrance to the doghouse, shards of white scattered among cedar chips. Quince tried to tell himself those weren't bones he was seeing. The stumps of his fingers throbbed. Blood trickled, spent. What the hell was he going to do? The gate was open, but he no longer had the strength to pull himself up.

The yard beyond was a blur of tears. Quince tried to focus, look for any sign of the girl. There was none.

He closed his eyes. The air felt warm on his face, comfortable. He shook himself. "Oh, no," he whispered. "No sleeping, now."

Nevertheless, the sensation of warmth filled him again. Quince fought to keep his eyes open, focusing on the trees, watching the dark leaves sway back and forth. From the distance drifted slow, desperate wails which Quince hoped were police sirens. Eventually his eyes closed and the old woman's yard disappeared.

About "Lavish"

Ah, "Lavish". So close to my heart, this. An epic tale if I ever wrote one. So much so that it became the basis for my novel *The Ark on the Common*, which I am currently marketing. But more on that in a moment.

Why "Lavish" for a title of a story dealing with a modern Great Flood? Friend and fellow writer Fran Bellerive had this idea-starter gimmick we used to use when we ran a writers group in Worcester years ago. You close your eyes, randomly open the dictionary and point. When you open your eyes you *have* to write something related to the word you've chosen. One day, the word was "Lavish". Aside from the usual meaning—*produced with extravagance and profusion, or immoderate in giving or bestowing*, the dictionary had a third definition: *a torrential downpour of rain.*

Well, that was a different enough to get the brain going. I though of floods, then the Great Flood. Where would one go to get away from a flood? The mountains. OK, the next question—and sometimes these *extra* questions we ask ourselves as writers make all the difference— what kind of flood could occur which would make even the mountains unsafe?

"Lavish" was born from the answer to this question. It's a modern take on the Great Flood. What if God tells thousands of people to build an ark, and wait for a new flood? These people have to convince others to help them, join their "crew" as it were. Not an easy task, I'd wager.

Now, a WARNING: as mentioned above, "Lavish" became my upcoming novel *The Ark on the Common*. "Lavish", barring obvious character differences and one significant event change, is the last chapter of the book. So if you'd rather wait, skip this little tale and come back here at a later date. Otherwise, I've kept the story as-is, without trying to incorporate any of the significant alterations inherent in the longer-form version.

LAVISH

They ascended the ramp two by two, not to honor any sense of history but from necessity. Husbands helped their wives along the narrow passage. Children ran on deck as if in a new playhouse. Unlike its predecessor, the vessel housed no animals. Exceptions were made for those who steadfastly refused to abandon pets.

Under white hot desert skies or snow-heavy clouds, the ships waited. They sat like sentinels not in water, but on grass or sand or rock. Two by two the passengers climbed atop their backs. The arks held them aloft above the laughter and derision of those gathered to watch.

*   *   *   *

"Mothers will cling to their babies and howl for mercy. One will scream *Take me but spare my child.* She will watch her innocent one disappear under the waves. In weakness and despair, she will know the ultimate horror, before falling into suffocating darkness herself."

The preacher's name was Jack. Like a scarecrow come to life, he moved through the crowd, joints popping in his knees as he twisted among the tourists standing in line for the ferry. Some feigned interest as they glanced nervously across the water towards the Statue of Liberty. Others stared in rapt fascination at the spectacle hobbling before them. Battery Park swarmed with a thousand souls, some vacationing, others eating business lunches from the multitude of hot dog and sausage carts. They were all a captive audience; Jack's impromptu parish.

As he preached, his eyes never focused on anyone in particular. From moment to moment he did not know where he stood or to whom he looked. God's words and vision flowed through his brain, slowly ripping him to shreds from the inside as he strove to open the minds and hearts of his audience.

"God's plans for me don't include survival. When the deluge comes, I will be cast into oblivion with the rest of you."

A murmur of disapproval rippled across the crowd. This pleased Jack. It meant they were listening. "Yes, that's right. We will die for certain when the flood comes. But if one of you can hear me, can heed God's words, then maybe what I say doesn't fall on barren ground."

"I heard you." The speaker was a young black man, stepping hesitantly forward from the crowd. He looked as thin as the preacher, all but lost within a New York Giants jacket made for colder seasons and larger physiques. "What are we supposed to do?"

Jack tried to blink away the sweat from his eyes. "You want to know what you can do?"

"Yes." The young man grabbed the preacher's hand. "Please tell us. Tell me."

Jack smiled. "There's nothing you can do." The grip on his hand tightened.

"First you say it's not too late. Now you're telling us we're going to die. Why don't you stop rambling like some crazy man and tell us what to do!"

Jack laughed, oblivious to the pain in his fingers. "There's nothing left to do. The end will come in a few minutes. You should have listened to me three months ago, when God's plan first revealed itself." He moved closer until their faces almost touched. He continued in a whisper, "But it's still not too late. Your body might perish but your soul's not yet dead."

The young man released Jack's hand and pushed him away. "You're nothing but a psycho. I'm sick of you and all the other Jesus freaks telling me I'm going to die. Maybe I should just kill you now." He grabbed Jack's shirt in two skinny handfuls. "Huh? Would you like that?"

Jack paid no attention as the young man tried to shake him. For the first time his eyes came completely into focus. He said, "There are others?"

*   *   *   *

Bernard Myers held a crystal glass in one hand and shaded his eyes with the other. Nothing hung over his head but distant wisps of clouds drifting over the Montana foothills. The eastern edge of the Rockies rose behind him, out of sight behind the crowded miles of forest. When his host resumed speaking, Bernard took a sip of his drink and tried to listen.

"I swear. They built an honest-to-God ark. If you take a right out of here and go for about twelve miles you'll see a Sunoco. Take a left at the next light and before you hit the town line, there it is." As he gave directions, Sanjiv gestured with the hand that held his beer, spilling some down his arm. "Right in the middle of the road. I'm not kidding. Not a bad job from what I can tell. There are hundreds of them all over the country. Everyone's nuts."

Bernard smiled but said nothing. At last count nearly three thousand arks had been constructed across the United States. Thousands more if one counted the rest of the world. Bernard didn't think this clarification would add anything to the conversation so he swirled his ice with an index finger and looked around the yard. A dozen guests in shorts or bathing suits wandered about the clearing. Bernard's wife Agnes moved from group to group. A thin white contrail marked her progress as she sucked the life out of yet another cigarette. The sky, reflected in the lake before them all, was as blue as yesterday and, if one believed the forecasts, as blue as tomorrow. Maybe everyone *was* nuts after all.

A hand squeezed his shoulder. "Bernie. Are you OK to drive? Karen and I would love to see the Ark, if you're up to driving two lonely girls all alone down some deserted road." As she spoke, Maureen pressed herself against his arm and leg. Bernard was pleased to find himself not wholly unaroused by the action. He glanced for a moment across the yard, at Agnes and her accompanying cloud.

"My dear, if I weren't so drunk I'd take you and your lovely friend on a trip you'd never forget." He raised his glass. "After the end of the world, perhaps?"

Maureen smiled and squeezed his arm. "It's a date."

Sanjiv finished his beer. "Speaking of Armageddon, how much longer do we have?"

Bernard checked his watch. "Twelve minutes, give or take."

Sanjiv moved to the center of the clearing. "Twelve minutes, everyone! If you have something you need to do on this earth you'd better do it now." He smiled as Karen and her husband raced towards the woods behind the cottage. The husband tried to run while fumbling with his sneaker. Karen ran past him, topless and waving a bra over her head like a banner. Maureen broke away from Bernard and raced in their direction.

"Hey, wait for me," she yelled, fumbling to raise the tee shirt over her head. Bernard watched her progress over the rim of his glass. He subtly turned his attention to Sanjiv, who no longer smiled but instead glared at the woman sitting alone at the end of the dock.

✷   ✷   ✷   ✷

Sitting upon a green sea of grass and dandelions, the ark was not that majestic symbol of nautical power depicted in countless historical paintings. Margaret smiled like a hostess greeting dinner guests. Her gaze kept returning to the gaps in the hull where uneven planks never quite came together. *God will keep us afloat*, she thought. At the top of the ramp Carl tucked the clipboard under his arm and leaned over the railing. At eighteen, his skin was a deep California bronze.

"That's it, Mrs. Carboneau," he shouted. "Full house. Maybe you should come aboard now? Everyone's heading below deck."

Carl was smiling, but Margaret heard his tension. Last night the Jorgensons haunted her with phone calls, asking why she was swallowing their son up in her madness. Each time she tried to explain that he approached her, not the other way around. She let them know she was not displeased with having him aboard, and would they reconsider and join him? It was a conversation repeated with so many others over the last three months. There had been some who seemed to believe what she told them. Rationalizing that a town eighty miles from the Pacific shoreline was in no danger of flooding, they weren't waiting below deck.

Time was up. Everyone onboard knew it. Or feared it. The true nature of their faith was not Margaret's business. She nodded at Carl and stepped onto the ramp. Someone grabbed the back of her shirt.

The woman looked only a few years older than Carl. It seemed as if she'd risen from bed minutes before. Her black hair fell in a mass of tangles over a faded blue sweatshirt. Margaret's attention was drawn to the baby which slept nestled against the shirt just below the Nike logo.

The woman said, "I hate to bother you like this."

Margaret smiled, making a conscious effort not to check her watch. Only a few minutes left, she knew.

"Can I help you?"

"I'm sorry. I was just wondering." She lowered her eyes and whispered, "Could you maybe fit my little boy and me on your boat? We'll be good. He's a very quiet baby." She looked up with eyes a mix of pride and desperation. "I know we had to sign up weeks ago, but I swear I can pay my way. I'm a nurse. I can cook, too, and I don't mind cleaning anything. Please, let us up."

Margaret's smile disappeared. Her first instinct was to hug the small family and walk them up the ramp. Then God's instructions came back to her. "I'm sorry," she whispered. "We can only fit a certain number of people. Any more will put everyone at risk." She put a hand on the woman's shoulder. "I'm sorry."

The young mother breathed quickly, rocking the baby deeper to sleep on her breast. Margaret wanted to run up the ramp and forget about this woman and her belated repentance. Her own daughters were waiting for her. "I'm sorry," she said again. "There isn't any more room."

The woman cried uninhibitedly now. Tears fell onto the baby, who squirmed and stretched defiantly in his sleep. "I'm sorry for not coming sooner. Please help us. Connor's just a baby. He doesn't deserve to die. Just take him, then. I don't matter. Please take my baby with you." She pressed him against Margaret's chest.

Margaret looked around the common. Small groups of spectators milled about, as if waiting for a band to begin playing. Families picnicked on the grass. She saw a woman pulling sandwiches from a plastic shopping bag while her three children thrashed about in some frenzied pre-lunch ritual. Any sympathy she held for them faded like a bad dream. They had been warned, but to them today was just another day. The young mother in front of her continued to offer up the baby for whatever salvation could be given. Margaret came to a sudden cold realization. There was something she could do. The thought sent her heart beating frantically in panic.

She gently pushed the child away. "A baby needs its mother."

The woman's horrified expression only made Margaret more convinced of her new course. Margaret looked up at Carl who still waited at the railing. He mouthed the words 'Come on....'

"Carl, can you ask Katie and Robin to come down here?"

At first Carl didn't respond. He looked at Margaret, then at the young mother and her baby. He slowly shook his head.

"Carl, please. We've got no more time left."

"Mrs. Car—"

"Please get them now." Her fear broke any attempt at a commanding voice. Carl waited another heart beat, then disappeared. The woman stopped crying, obviously struggling to understand what was happening. Margaret did not look at her. In a minute Carl returned with Katie and Robin. The two girls raced each other down the ramp and grabbed Margaret's legs.

Katie was the oldest by three years and a foot taller than her sister. She smiled and said, "Mom, when are you coming up?"

Margaret kneeled on both knees. "I'm not, honey," she whispered. "We're going to help this lady and her baby. It's what Jesus taught us to do. I think he wants us with Him in heaven real soon."

Robin smiled as only a three-year-old could. She stood on her toes and hugged Margaret's neck. "You mean it? Are we going to see Daddy?"

Katie did not smile. She sidled closer to her mother. Looking sharply at the older daughter in a silent warning, Margaret said to Robin, "I hope so baby. I'm sure we'll see him soon."

"Ma'am?" the woman said, then swallowed. Her expression matched that of Katie: a slowly developing horror at what was unfolding before her. "I don't understand." But she did.

"Go on up. A mother should stay with her baby."

"Mom?"

"Hush a moment."

Baby Connor's eyes were now open. He stared up at his mother, offering the beginnings of a smile. "I can't—" She did not finish the sentence. Both knew it would have been a lie.

"Go now. Please. Time is up. Go right now."

The woman pulled the baby close and ran up the plank. She disappeared on deck behind Carl.

"Mrs. Carboneau. You can't let her on." Margaret ignored him and turned to Katie. The girl's face was wet with tears.

"Katie, there's still room for you on the boat."

"Mom, I don't want to leave you."

"It's up to you. Please think carefully. You'll have to stay down here if you don't go on board." On the surface it was a painfully obvious statement. Margaret knew this was too much for a six-year old to decide, but at this point she wondered how clearly any of them were thinking.

"I don't want to die!"

"Hush."

"Mom, are we going to die?"

Margaret took both girls' hands in her own. "God will take us into his arms and keep us safe. He loves us."

Katie leaned against her mother, intelligent eyes scanning Margaret's face. Robin did the same, hoping the imitation would help her understand her sister's fear. Katie said, "Mom, I don't want to go back on the boat without you."

"Then stay here with me. I'll hold you close." To her surprise, Katie stayed.

They sat together on the grass, the two girls fidgeting on her lap. Margaret looked up. "Drop the ramp, Carl."

"No."

"Drop it, Carl. We're out of time."

* * * *

Nicole dipped her toes in the water. The midday sun exploded in short bursts from the ripples. She heard Sanjiv shout his twelve-minute warning. The couple standing on the dock behind her walked slowly towards his voice. Nicole was left alone. She shivered though the sun had burned down on her all morning.

Bernard walked slowly along the dock until he stood beside her. He looked at the sky and took another sip from the glass. All he got was a small sliver of ice cube.

"Your husband throws quite a party," he said. Nicole did not speak. Bernard turned back to face the cottage. From this vantage, he had a partly obstructed view of the threesome in the woods: white skin rolling and curving in the shade. He sighed and looked at his hostess. "What are you doing?"

Nicole made more ripples and said, "Praying."

Bernard raised an eyebrow, though the effect was lost on the woman as she continued staring at the lake splashing over her toes. He said, "Not taking any chances, are we?"

Nicole stopped her silent musings and looked up "I'm praying because I was told to."

"By God?"

"Yes." Her embarrassment at the confession only served to soil her mood further. How could she be so concerned what this man thought? There were others screaming on every street corner who weren't ashamed. She couldn't help but think of the message given to her by God as deeply personal.

She looked past Bernard's legs to her husband, who laughed and drank with his guests. He caught her gaze for a moment then as quickly looked away. She'd told him about the vision after it had come to her three months ago. He needed to know what would happen. But Sanjiv had laughed and ended the conversation. Since then he avoided any discussion of floods, or God in general. Eventually she stopped bringing the subject up. Soon after that, the visions stopped.

Now everyone was here at their postcard-perfect cottage, mocking her and her short-lived gift of sight. That wasn't quite true, she supposed. Sanjiv likely never mentioned his wife's premonitions to anyone. Last night he warned her not to bring it up at the party. So she didn't. He was the only one who could know what this party meant to her. Nicole wondered if being beaten by your husband could be worse than this.

Bernard said something, but she could not make out his words. Something buzzed in her ears. She slapped at the air, then stopped with her arm in mid swing. A terrible certainty took hold of her.

"It's time," she said.

Bernard did not reply. He looked skyward. Nothing but a deep blue all around. And around. And around.

Bernard fell to the deck then into the lake. He thrashed at the surface, letting go of his glass. He tried to get a footing on the muddy lake bed but for the moment could not decide which way was down. The beach and dock seemed to heave and spin over him. He wondered vaguely how much he had drunk. Then the water wrapped itself around him in a swirling undertow and pulled him away from shore. The sky tumbled below him. With a panicked thrash he broke through the surface, only to see trees then a road roll above him.

Lying face down on the dock, Nicole splayed her fingers wide. Her legs dangled in the water but the rest of her body pressed against the wood. She tried to breathe. The world pulled at her from every conceivable direction, but something held her in place. She felt the water reach past her knees like a monster under the bed, grabbing her. Then the water raced away. Her legs shot out behind, desperate to follow. She remained pressed against the boards, gulping air into her compressed lungs. She hadn't noticed Bernard Myers racing away in the retreating water.

* * * *

No sound traveled into space. Earth in its tremendous majesty hung somewhere within the deep silence. Its perpetual rotation was a constant, unnoticed against the backdrop of infinity. Also unnoticed was the sudden interruption in this rotation.

Like a child's toy on a string, the blue and white planet stopped spinning. It remained motionless for only a moment. As Nicole struggled for breath against the dock and Bernard Myers released his empty glass into the lake, the massive planet began its rotation once more, in the opposite direction.

*   *   *   *

Slowly, the pressure holding everyone to the pavement subsided. As it did, Battery Park was filled with the sound of hundreds of people heaving gasps of air into their lungs. Jack grabbed the railing. An inner joy verging on ecstasy spun in his mind, more than the vertigo that had seized them all. *God is truth*, he thought. *His word is truth and He has delivered unto us His promise.*

He wiped his eyes so he could see God's destruction clearly. Across the water, the Statue of Liberty was not a crumbling pile of metal and stone. It held its stained torch to the sky. Jack rubbed his eyes again. Something was happening. The screams of those behind him were overpowered by the roaring of the churning bay. Waves smashed into others crashing upon the eroded shore of Liberty Island. Jack raised his arms.

"Behold," he shouted, "God's final—" Then he stopped. Like a leashed dog watching his master's car drive away Jack watched the waters of New York Bay smash and roar away from him in a reverse flood. The ferries with their screaming passengers were swept away, as if a plug had been pulled from some massive drain far out to sea. Jack fell against the railing, his mind confused by the sight. Miles away the bay surged with a momentum built over millions of years, up the shores then completely over Staten Island.

Along the milky horizon, the Atlantic Ocean moved like a fading gray wall eastward, then was gone.

Someone struck him on the shoulder. Jack did not turn around. People grabbed his arms and hands; some with violence, others pleading.

"You son of a bitch," a man's voice spat. "What did you do?"

"Please, it's not too late, I know it isn't. Please touch me and bless me."

Jack did not listen to their words. He stared across the glistening canyon of mud. He whispered to the lost sea. "Come back. Please come back to me."

"Turn around, you coward."

"Forgive me, father...."

"Make it stop. Make it stop, please make it stop."

Jack's grip on the railing fell away. Pulled and guided and shoved into the throng of his self-proclaimed parish, he floated away on their hands and arms. He stared past the bobbing heads, into the sky. In a sea of a hundred faces that twisted and writhed into their own distinct emotion, Jack never felt more alone.

*   *   *   *

When she was able, Margaret gathered Robin and Katie back into to her arms. "Come here. Stay close," she said. She could not hear her own words. Behind, what had begun a few seconds earlier as a low rumbling intensified in volume. The ramp still led up to the ark from the grass. Carl was slowly pulling himself up with the railing.

Margaret shouted louder with every word. "Drop the ramp, Carl. Do it now." Wind blew with a panicked force against her back. Twisting along with it, or perhaps pushing it along, the roaring din sounded like a freight train storming out of control towards them.

Carl knelt by the bolts holding the ramp in place. He looked at Margaret. Again she yelled, "Drop it Carl, for God's sake...." Her words were lost in the wind.

Katie cringed, more at her mother's tone than words. The situation became all too clear in her mind. Instead of standing and running up the ramp like she wanted to do, she wrapped her arms around Margaret's neck. It was then that she saw what was coming towards them.

Carl looked nervously around the perimeter of the boat. In blind unison, the spectators converged on the ark. Carl's gaze fell to Margaret's face. Her panicked expression shook him loose from his stupor. From the west, something massive was filling the sky. He saw but did not think about it. He pulled the bolts. The ramp fell with a thud onto the grass.

The mob slammed against the hull. Men in suits tried to scale the greased sides, only to slip and fall onto three others waiting below. The woman with the sandwiches raised one of her children towards the deck. There was no one there to lift him up.

Carl slammed the bulkhead and bolted it with one motion. He jumped the last three steps and stopped. In the sunlight streaming through the gaps in the hull, he made out the young woman whom Margaret had sent up the ramp. She wandered with her baby among the confused gazes of the passengers, shouting something he could not hear over the mind-rattling roar of the approaching water. He pushed her towards Margaret's vacant spot in the middle of the boat. Without any other thought but the routine they had all rehearsed a hundred times prior, he tied her arms and legs against beam. At first she would not release the child, but with as much delicacy as possible Carl wrenched young Connor from her and secured him as best he could in the harness originally slotted for Robin. The baby squirmed and cried. Carl felt his own chest heaving with sobs he couldn't hear. The entire boat shook. Whatever it was would hit them in seconds. He tried to pull the baby free and though the harness bounced and stretched, it did not release its grip. It would have to do.

The outside daylight faded. Carl looked across the floor to where his harness hung empty. He wasn't going to make it.

The sound, reflected in the screaming face of her oldest daughter, was the sound of surf magnified a million times. Katie gripped her neck so tightly Margaret gasped for breath. On her lap, Robin's mouth moved calmly in song. Margaret wished she could hear it. She stared at the child's lips and watched her sing to the wind.

Behind the fire station a wall of uncountable leagues of salt water rose from the western horizon. The sun reflected off its face in immense ribbons of swirling color. Ahead of it all came the wind like a trumpeting angel, and the deafening sound of a thousand million high tides rolling towards shore but never cresting.

As Carl ran for his harness and Margaret stared transfixed at her baby's song, a shadow passed over the common. Then, like so many chess pieces, the trees and buildings and people were swept away.

*   *   *   *

Arms flailing wildly, Carl hovered in the middle of the ark as it rolled over and around him. The darkness was nearly complete, except for the occasional shadow whirling overhead. He could make out voices. Some were screams but others were calm, directed to children and pets alike as everyone hollered or barked or mewed in terror. Carl felt as if he'd been tossed into a madman's carnival ride. He expected to be deluged in water, but felt nothing but an icy wind tearing through the gaps in the hull.

He sensed the beam before he actually hit it, a dark foreboding shape rising from the gloom below. He raised his left arm. When they connected, it was the arm that gave way. A bright flash filled his vision. His body went limp and rolled away from the beam in time with the tumbling of the ship. He landed on someone's chest. Two heavy fists gathered him up by the tee-shirt and pulled him close. His legs tumbling behind him, Carl reached for his left arm. Something hard and jagged protruded just above the elbow. Touching it sent a vibration coursing through his body. He realized what he held between his fingers was a jagged edge of bone. Feeling on his face the hot breath of whoever held him, he passed out.

* * * *

Gravity pulled at the heaving surge of water as if to reclaim a lost toy. By the time the ocean reached the Rocky Mountains it was no more than a mile higher than the tallest peak. As the wave rolled across the mountains its underbelly tore open. The wave crested. Miles of sea, rock and ice curved in on itself and fell to earth, like a giant on a toppling beanstalk.

* * * *

Bernard Myers stared at the sky. Clouds raced by, stretched thin by the wind. Though nothing seemed to be pinning him down, he could move neither his legs nor his arms. The house he'd glimpsed before the lake cast him down was gone. Shattered beams and even a bathtub rose in his peripheral vision. He wondered if the wooden stake protruding from some numb area of his lower body was once part of the same house. He also wondered if his back was broken.

From his vantage, Bernard could see the Rocky Mountains to the west. They rose high over the trees that once blocked his view. A blurred gray bank of clouds rose quickly over the snow-capped peaks. It spread north and south as far as his paralyzed gaze could see. *So the final storm approaches*, he mused. Thunder rolled steady and unending over him.

The rising cloud bank draped over the mountains. Bernard watched brilliant streaks of white rip into the gray blanket. What he had originally took for thunder intensified, then he understood. The cloudburst everyone had waited for was come and gone. The flood waters left in their wake advanced with a speed Bernard could not begin to measure.

God, I'm sorry for every bad thing I did. I've never been to confession, as you probably know, but...oh hell. He sighed. Air gurgled in his lungs. *Forget about me. Take care of Aggie. Please. She can be a royal pain in the ass sometimes, but she's a good woman.* He watched with resigned dispassion the approaching monster.

* * * *

Agnes stumbled across the yard, fumbling with her lighter. When she finally ignited the cigarette on the ninth try the smoke burst from her mouth only to be whisked across the empty lake. Fueled by the nicotine she ran towards the cottage shouting, "Bernie? Bernie?" No one paid her any heed. They gazed through their own fearful stupor at the lake or the sky or each other.

Sanjiv stood at the edge of the grass, one foot tentatively on the dock. He stared down its length to Nicole, who hung awkwardly from the edge. The ground shook in chorus with the baleful roar approaching from behind. He bit his tongue to keep the growing hysteria from showing in his face. He felt betrayed, but could not understand why. Somehow all of this, foretold in her god-forsaken premonitions, seemed to be Nicole's fault. She was making this happen.

He never believed in God, no more now than when Nicole first started her religious ravings. Wrapped up in the sound and wind Sanjiv wanted to believe in God and heaven and hell more than he remembered wanting anything before. He began walking towards her. It was then, in the last five seconds of his life Sanjiv knew what he had to do. Kill the woman and stop the madness.

Nicole watched Sanjiv watching her. She wondered if he noticed the vomit on her shirt. Her husband's face twitched with an effort to appear emotionless. She'd seen him do this so many times before. Now, though, a thin line of blood seeped from the corner of his mouth. Sanjiv's eyes never wavered from hers. Nicole's hands ached. She now slipped past the edge of the wood, keeping her head above the dock as if treading water. The mud at the bottom of the pier sucked at her ankles.

"I'm sorry," she said. Like Agnes' smoke, Nicole's voice tore away behind her. Sanjiv must have seen her lips move for he spoke as well. She was grateful not to hear him. He reached the end of the dock.

Reflexively Nicole released her grip. She sank to her knees, wondering if she would go right on sinking, falling away from the man leaning over her. The trees, cottage and earth holding them all in place erupted. Sanjiv never looked back. The world seemed suspended in that final moment as he leaned further and reached towards his wife. The destruction whirled behind him in a quickly descending backdrop. Then the Pacific Ocean slammed them all into oblivion.

* * * *

The first crest rolled over the Rocky Mountain valleys. In a mad game of leap frog the next wave tumbled over the malay. Torn between gravity and momentum it found its mark sixty miles further east. In this manner the water moved from town to town and state to state. Each cresting wave surged lower than its predecessor until the sea, its initial enthusiasm spent, rolled slowly across the Plains. It settled miles deep, then less, then simply spread as a level of rising salt water that broke and fell back against the first significant obstacle in its path.

At its furthest point, just east of the Mississippi River, the flood became a playground for children who understood little its source. They danced in the salty puddles; scooped mud into red plastic buckets. Trembling on porches their mothers and fathers stared westward and wondered why they had been spared. They sat in folding chairs and watched increasing numbers of pale green helicopters thumping with an angry urgency towards the distant western hills.

* * * *

The sail flapped uncertainly in the wind. On his knees, Carl leaned against the railing and stared at the sea. Now and then the sleek body of a dolphin broke the surface as it swam westward, following the receding tide. Not for the first time, Carl wondered why it was Margaret he searched for among the waves, rather than his own family. He tried to imagine what his parents went through in those final moments, but all he could summon was a still image of his front yard. The only reality he could imagine at the moment was Margaret, and he knew now she was gone forever. He thought about a discussion they had two weeks ago. Did she believe in the Rapture, when God would take his chosen ones body and soul to heaven before sending his punishment? She laughed at the question. The way she saw it, why would God choose so many people for this grand adventure then spoil their fun at the last minute?

Now Carl wondered once more. Milling around the ship, the passengers gazed across the water, or kept their children busy with games and stories. No one prayed. No one seemed to know what they should be doing. At that last moment before he dropped the ramp, Carl looked at Margaret and her children sitting on the grass and thought *They're the only ones who deserve to be on this ship and they're sitting on the ground waiting to die.* Now they were gone, leaving the survivors to sort things out for themselves.

Maybe the Rapture had come after all.

"You should sleep for a while. If there's anyone out there they can get you to a hospital and set this arm right." She didn't say the rest ("If there are any hospitals left") but he could hear it in her voice nonetheless.

The baby lay on its belly and sucked on the edge of a blanket. The woman checked the splint on Carl's arm. She had been a nurse after all. When the ship stopped its rolling and broke into daylight, she immediately took charge of setting the bone back into place. Since then she hadn't left his side. She even fed young Connor on her breast in front of him. It was a fitting penance for taking the Carboneaus' place, Carl assumed. He turned from the railing. The deck was still wet and soaked his pants when he sat. With the baby at his feet, Carl tried to sleep.

Across the new landscape, the makeshift fleet turned its bows toward the sun. They followed its burning light as it fell behind the eastern horizon. Reds and yellows spread like fire across the water. The people sailed the ships as best they could against the wind, and waited for someone to come.

About "The Storm of Generations"

I love Ray Bradbury. OK, so I've never actually *met* Mr. Bradbury, but I love his writing, both in content and style. I keep one particular non-fiction book of his on the window sill beside my bed. It's a tiny collection of essays called *The Zen of Writing*, a must-read for anyone who strives to do the fantastic-fiction thing.

In one particular essay, Bradbury talks of how he would think of a word or two and let it roll around in his head. He would type the word on a piece of paper. Then, he would type a few more related words, seeing what comes of it (go buy the book and read it yourself before I completely bastardize the Master's essay).

One night I decided to try it. It was *literally* a Dark and Stormy Night, lightening flashing behind the window shade, Big Booms of Thunder, rain, rain, rain. I typed "Rain". I typed "Storm", then "Clouds". I wrote an introductory paragraph about a young couple sitting on a hillside watching a storm roll towards them. Since I'm a mondo Spielberg fan, I had the boy mention that something was coming for them in the clouds. The storm rolls over them, and I continued with a twisted alien abduction scene which never made it into the final draft of the story. I stopped when the girl wakes up on the hillside and the boy is gone.

I had no idea what came next, except that I wanted this to be a quiet story about a quiet invasion, so I shelved the story and waited. One day, out of the blue, I think, *She's Pregnant. All the men are gone and all the woman are pregnant.* I eventually changed the concept to only having sixteen-year-old girls being pregnant, because otherwise there would be mass chaos nine months later.

Like "Lavish", I have a feeling that this story might someday become a novel. For now, though, here it is:

The Storm of Generations

Distant electricity turned the grass a shimmering green. On the hillside, the young couple sat among the foot-high blades. Clouds bulged, rolled and collapsed, perhaps a mile out.

"They're coming," Jared muttered as he bit off another chunk of bread. An avalanche of crumbs fell into his lap.

"No one's coming. It's a thunderstorm. Nothing special about it."

Jared didn't reply, but stared with a growing restlessness at the thunderheads. They loomed closer, a moment later seemed to pull away. A vague sense of vertigo washed over him. He looked at Serena, wanted to touch her again. Just her shoulder, hard skin through the cotton blouse. No sense starting something he couldn't finish. Not with whatever lurked inside those clouds getting closer.

He shook his head and took another bite of bread.

The air smelled faintly of iron. It reminded Serena of the time she licked the end of a C battery. Living metal. According to Jared, a ship sailed in those clouds. Maybe more than one.

"I was right about passing the physics final," he said, "wasn't I? Same way I know about this. Dreams, Sen. Dreams don't lie." He leaned back in the grass, as if offering himself to the approaching invaders, and folded his arms behind his head. "Don't you smell it? Christ, I can feel the things from here."

Serena couldn't tell how serious Jared took his premonitions. She pulled her legs up, locked them in place with her arms. The act wasn't born out of any insecurity around her boyfriend's prediction, but, rather, from a sudden gust racing up the hillside. It was the middle of June. The humidity atomized from the approaching electricity, the barometer crashing into its bulbous cellar.

Jared had a dream he would be taken away this afternoon. Serena's father woke up last night. He may have shouted. Layers of sheets and the half-closed door muted her parents' voices. She thought she had heard her father crying.

Gooseflesh on her arms. What made pre-thunderstorm air so cool, so clean? The two sat in silence on the grass, waiting for the first blade of lightening to break their reverie and send them scurrying for cover. She rested her chin on denim knees and stared at the storm. It dropped down on them like a rogue ocean wave.

White.

A blank wall. Or a ceiling.

She'd been hit by lightening. This was a hospital. But where'd she been three minutes ago? One, six. No existence before this. Was it only a dream, sitting on the hillside with Jared, watching the clouds? The room spun. Serena watched herself come apart, fall back together.

She was sixteen. What did that have to do with anything?

Fuzzy shapes flittered about. She tried to kick. Nothing moved. She had no legs.

"Serena." Jared's voice. She couldn't feel her hands. Had they been stolen, too?

Jared was close.

As soon as this thought came to her, the sensation disappeared forever.

* * * *

"Grandma?" Serena looked up. She'd been dozing again.

Lucille stood on the single step leading from the porch to the front yard. Her dress already bore three new stains since breakfast. Serena checked her watch. Church started in twenty minutes and Alice's little girl already looked unkempt. Serena smiled at her great-great-granddaughter and shuffled forward in the wicker chair.

"Come here, Cutie." She smoothed the dress over her lap. Lucille skipped onto the porch and clambered up. Serena held her close. Reverend Corinne wouldn't be happy, seeing the Daws clan skulk into their pew, once again after the procession was already up the aisle.

Nothing to do about it now. Lucille snuggled against her Grandma's neck. Down the sloping lawn, the silver spaceship sat all but ignored at the bottom of the hill. It crouched, an echo of a nightmare never fully dissipated. Six legs jutted in right angles from the body, straddling Barber's Brook. A massive bug forever poised to strike, unchanged in every way for the last fifty-one years.

"Grandma?" Lucille referred to all her grandparents that way. Everyone did. "Grandma" or "Nana." Serena preferred "Grandma," so that's what they used. "Grandma Serena," "Grandma Jane."

"Grandma Maura." Maura had marked the half-way point in the line. Little Lucille's grandmother, Serena's grand daughter. Maura died in a plane crash when she was eighteen, finally taking her belated post-natal vacation. She'd chosen Washington. The government complied, even paid her way. A small price for her contribution to the population. Fate, however, did not comply. Fortunately, the Line wasn't severed. Baby Alice, then two years old, was the continuation. And continue it did. Lucille was talking. Serena looked at her and tried to recall what the girl had just said. No use. She smiled instead.

"Hmm?"

"I said, are you coming to my recital? Mommy bought me a new dress."

* * * *

Cool grass on her face. Rain drops across her back. Dizzying, this sensation of water falling in minute explosions on and around her. She lay prone on the hillside, among tall blades of grass, taking inventory of her body. Jeans in tact. No socks anymore, white tennis sneakers. Had she worn socks today? Maybe not. Muscles felt heavy like her wet clothes.

Details of the clouds blurred to an undefined haze as rain stretched across the town.

"Jared?"

How long had she been out? Hit by lightening. Yes, of course. But not dead. Serena squinted away the rain and looked behind her, up the short distance to the rise. Two intertwined hemlocks offered futile shelter from the storm. She looked back down through the haze. Something long and silver squatted in the distance, near a cluster of trees at the curve of Devonshire Road. Something fluttered in her belly, like the loose edges of nerves she tried to tie before each year's dance recital. Serena looked once more around the hillside, trying to remember what she was looking for.

Then it came to her. Jared was gone.

* * * *

"Is that a man?" Jane let go of her mother's hand, shuffled towards the painting as if hypnotized. Before them, a sixteenth century orgy spread out, all motion and color. Four men and five woman lounged among each other's limbs, all naked but for an occasional loose tunica—a celebratory salute to the pleasures of the flesh. Always the ode to Bacchus, Serena noted, a whisper of melancholy playing across her face. She missed Jared. Not just because of what they'd shared together. Physically, it wasn't a whole lot. What would their world have been like, if things hadn't gone to shit? What would have happened, if the two had reached this dream-like point? Jared holding her, like the Bacchus-image holding the woman. Was this scene real, or some painter's lurid fantasy? Men and woman. The possibilities seemed endless.

"Mommy?"

Serena swallowed. "Yes. Those are men."

Jane paused for a moment, then pointed at a flailing penis. "Is that a—"

"Yes," Serena said, hoping the interruption would throw some discouragement her daughter's way, at least with this particular topic. Maybe later. Not in front of the painting.

Jane stared for a while, moving now and again to a new vantage point. Nine year-old girls had their own methodical rhythm. They seemed to ponder everything, turning things over inexhaustibly, finishing in their own time. "Did Daddy have one?" she finally said.

Daddy; meaning Jared, of course. As if a virgin birth were some horrifying label to be peeled away. As if it didn't happen to every sixteen year-old girl these days. As soon as she could listen, Jane learned about her father, about Jared. Serena even named her after him, as close a name as she could come up with. She never truly explained to her daughter what "father" meant. What did it matter? It wasn't a necessary part of the equation anymore.

"Yes, he had one."

Jane made a face and turned away. "Gross."

*   *   *   *

Women gathered on the south end of Devonshire Road, to get a better look at the wonder everyone called "the bug." Serena's nausea abated, retreating after a reluctant breakfast of butterless toast and water. The fourth morning waking up like this.

No word from her father. No word from her brothers. And no Jared. All gone. Every man on the planet replaced, it seemed, by these squatting alien monuments.

Serena's mother refused to come out of the bedroom.

With nothing else to do, only CNN and the local PBS station back on line, Serena followed the growing crowd as it moved purposely along Marjorie Drive, then Devonshire. Leading the mob, the woman who tried to get her mother into Amway two years ago. Mrs. Kyle stood an easy four inches over the next tallest woman in the group. Black hair shot tightly back in a bun, she looked like an old-fashioned school marm searching out delinquent students. She shrieked, "They're in there!"

Everyone followed her vindictive finger towards the ship. "All of them. My boys." She looked at Susan Miller. "And, Sue, your husband, too. All of your husbands." The finger scanned the uneasy group. "All of your sons."

Serena expected the crowd to start gathering up stones. Yet everyone knew better. In fact, warning the remaining population about the ships' defenses seemed the sole impetus for CNN's return two days earlier. Mrs. Kyle continued her pleas. "We have to get this thing open. Those warnings are bull shit! The government doesn't want us too close, to find out what's really inside."

She reached for Susan Miller's arm, but the woman jerked back like a shell-shocked dog. "Those things are booby trapped," Susan hissed. "You damn well know that. You saw the vid—"

"Special effects." Mrs. Kyle walked confidently up to the ship, bent her head towards the hull's polished surface. "Andy?" She called like a lover outside a bedroom window. To Serena she sounded like a frightened Aunt Bea. "Andy? Jimmy? You boys are in there. I know you're in there." She leaned closer and whispered, "You knew they were coming. Somehow...." The words clouded her reflection. Serena felt a chill along her arms, remembering her father's nightmare, Jared's calm certainty.

Mrs. Kyle turned her head, perhaps to scan the faces in the crowd. The tight bun of hair brushed against the ship, lightly as her breath. "See?" she said. "Am I dead y—"

It took Serena's brain a few seconds to figure out what it was seeing. By the time the woman's head and right shoulder were shredded into something resembling spaghetti, Serena was stumbling away, fighting once more to hold down the toast.

* * * *

Two or three blurred shapes moved around her, pulled away. The fuzzy outline at the foot of the bed said, "Grandmother Serena? Are you all right?"

Serena tried to focus. Her heart beat with less regularity these days. Now it strained with fear. Not of the shapes. If she had her glasses they would come back into focus. The fear, maybe apprehension was a better word, revolved around the nightmare. And her daughters. Her daughter; the rest were daughters' daughters.

From the moment of that final push to bring Jane into the world, Serena Daws tried to live with a lie. Soon all of the lost pieces would fall back into place like a celestial jigsaw. Sixteen years and two months after that lie began, Serena's teenage daughter woke up pregnant. Holding grandchild Maura in her arms, Jane sleeping out her exhaustion on the hospital bed, Serena accepted with resigned clarity that the world no longer belonged to her. She was a guest in someone else's home. Not a single male of the species remained, nor would ever return. The illusion, the lie, fell away, overpowered by her granddaughter's newborn cries. The iron storm which rolled across the hill, years before, scraped away Serena's universe and replaced it with something half-done. Or so it seemed then. The Earth did vibrate with a much calmer frequency. There hadn't been a single war, not since half the population was taken. Borders were dissolving, reforming into new patterns.

Still, Serena found herself standing before paintings or watching old movies, vying for a glimpse of what might have been. What had been. Now, she lay in bed and reflected, as if to pull some spiritual circle closed.

"Grandmother Serena? Can you hear me?" The fuzzy shape was Art. She, the only one of Serena's Line who used the formal "Grandmother" instead of "Grandma".

"I'm fine, Art. Just a bad dream."

She fumbled with her glasses, managed to wrangle them on. Still, Art was a blur, as were the other two figures beside the bed. One of them took Serena's pulse. Perhaps the doctor. Lately, everyone had lost their edges, become blurred photographs of the originals. This current pair of glasses was less than a year old, and already useless.

Dreams were the only part of her life still sharply in focus. The same dream, since the day her neighbor got minced by the bug. It returned in one form or another, now and again. Lately, once or twice a week. She stood at the side of Devonshire Road, sometimes alone, sometimes with other faceless women. Always, Mrs. Kyle, slamming her fists against the body of the ship. Some dreams ended as reality had, the angry woman coming apart as if tossed against fan blades. At other times, like tonight, Mrs. Kyle succeeded. Her fingers gripped an invisible fault in the bug's hull. A large rectangular door clanged onto the pavement. Liquefied remains of Jared and a thousand other men poured from the ship's intestines. Sewerage spilling from an open pipe. Brown and crimson. Excrement washing across everyone's feet. Jared's pained expression floated among the flotsam toward the sewer drain.

*   *   *   *

Brenda Singleton examined a box of Saltine crackers with pale distaste. Serena rolled her shopping cart alongside. They exchanged small talk, then symptoms. Around them, a dozen others silently collected groceries, for the most part taking only what they really needed. The supermarket opened now for six hours a day, everyone taking turns maintaining what dwindling stock remained until the proverbial supply chain could wind itself back up. Every cash register was unattended.

Serena's attention locked onto the home pregnancy test sitting on the pita bread in Brenda's cart.

"Oh, my God, Bren. How...I mean, no not how...I mean I know how. Who's the...." But the question died away.

Brenda looked at her with undisguised terror. "There is no father," she said, dropping the box of crackers beside the tester.

Serena whispered, "There has to be a father." When she reached the aisle with the pregnancy tests, only two kits remained.

*   *   *   *

The intangible shape of Art leaned over, laid on an extra blanket. Serena liked the way names were going lately. Art would be pregnant any month now, and her daughter's name would be Time. Art was like that, choosing the name early, always planning.

This would be Serena's death bed. Resigned acceptance once again. But it was about time. Ninety-eight years felt to her a good enough span. Most of Serena's original class had already moved on, accompanied by a flourish of mourning and remembrance from their lineage. Honoring each departing member of the "First Generation." No doubt Serena's own clan would do the same. What then?

The world would move on. Babies would be born. Young girls playing in the grass without fear, never thinking of boys. Waiting with eager longing for their sixteenth birthday. How long would the cycle continue? She'd taken to obsessing over this question. Maybe the pattern would carry on, long enough to populate the world with whomever, or whatever, rolled over the hillside all those years ago.

She closed her eyes and felt a cool cloth touch her forehead. Her children did appreciate the role their original grandmother played, unwitting as it was, in their existence. They looked upon the dying first generation with a reverence once reserved for royalty.

Serena felt herself sink into sleep. Maybe the nap would be her last, maybe not. She felt a sense of comfort, knowing that when the moment came her family would surround her. These were the generations Serena Daws had raised and loved. More would surely come without her.

About "Two Fish to Feed the Masses"

OK. So I finally caved and wrote a zombie story. There was a pretty big anthology calling for these stories a while back and I decided, at writer Paul Tremblay's suggestion, to give it a shot. In the end, though the editor tried to hold onto it as long as possible, it was too close in theme to another story from a volume of stories he'd previously published. *Sigh*. This happens. So much for being original. I considered marketing it elsewhere, but when a themed anthology closes up shop, there's usually a glut of similarly-themed stories hitting editors' desks, so since I was putting this collection together anyway, it's always good to have some original pieces included.

After you read this story you'll understand what I mean when I say it was written during a particular Crisis of Faith. I was basically yelling (read as *whining*) to God about stuff, mostly around my writing…we do that a lot, argue I mean.

I started this story not really knowing where I was going with it. I started with a character much like one named Jack from "Lavish", preaching in an empty street. As I went along, things started to develop. In re-reading this baby, there's a lot of various themes I ended up sticking in there—zombies, of course, the Rapture, (though I hadn't realized *Left Behind* had that kid-angle until I recently read the book) and Richard Matheson's classic *I Am Legend*. I was probably thinking of the latter when I made the zombies nocturnal.

The title, by the way, is in reference to the story of Jesus feeding hundreds of people who'd come to listen to Him with only a few loaves of bread and a couple of fish. This is one example of a story not having a title until the thing was finished.

Two Fish to Feed the Masses

"They stared at you and did not blink. They showed you what lust and greed would give if only you looked deeper into their deception! If only you tore open your souls and let them lick you clean like ravenous harlots. They damned you!"

The last two words echoed off the buildings, then carried back over Dinneck. He paused, listening to God's words drift behind the abandoned Federal Reserve building towards the Atlantic. Words were food, to be diluted, perhaps, in water. Two fish could feed millions, the book said. Now the seas overflowed with manna that no one would eat.

"No one to eat of God's bounty," he whispered, then remembered his place, his role in this final safe hour of afternoon. He raised his arms, his voice. The Boston skyline reached up to the abandoned heavens with him.

"It's not too late to salvage your souls, stolen by the Face! That which is taken can always be regained." As he spoke, Dinneck walked slowly from South Station, knowing his words echoed in the vast halls of the subway below. He hoped they did not fall on barren ground.

Christ the King church was a good half hour walk. Best to be cautious since his watch battery died. Time did not matter, only the setting of the sun. The Shufflers' pack mentality could corner any living person too foolish to properly plan an escape route away from their slow, methodical snares. Even overcast days were spent indoors. The Runners dared not risk such gloom, but the Shufflers were too stupid to know the difference between the murk of twilight and a thick-clouded storm blowing past. This fact made the Shufflers no less dangerous, unless the sun broke through. Then, Dinneck would walk among the fallen shells of their bodies, eyes smoking, contrails of their captive souls burned free into the air.

Dinneck would avoid these unfortunates if he came across them. They were dead, of course, insides decaying slowly in crusted shells that once were skin. They were dead *before* the sun broke through the clouds. But the demons within them, stupid, growling slugs never quite adapting to their new forms might linger still, looking for a new host. These victims of the sun were always gone in the morning. The Runners were efficient that way, as if leaving their lost brethren to lay in the street might make the New Race look bad.

Shufflers. Runners. New Race.

That night Dinneck reviewed the names in his notebook as he sat in the church pew. Candlelight licked across his *New Race Dictum* as if to consecrate the work. He preached by day, begging Hell-imprisoned souls to fight back, reclaim what had been stolen from them. By night, he documented the world as it was, after the Face reached into every house and stole so many away.

* * * *

"Dad, Dad! Come on, hurry! You can't miss the first five minutes or nothing will make sense! Everyone says that! Hurry!"

"That's OK. I'm recording it. I really have to finish this or Bert'll have my butt. You and Mom watch it tonight. If you want to watch it again with me tomorrow night you can tell me when the good parts are coming."

Nicky's expression passed from sorrowful hurt to hopeful expectation. "You promise? Really promise?"

At that moment Albert Dinneck almost—almost—said to hell with Bert and his deadlines. He'd get the galley revisions in a day later. Still, they were already a *month* late, and tomorrow was "Do or die, Buddy Boy" if *Eyes Closed* was to make Christmas. After tonight, the novel would be done and Albert could focus all of himself on Nicky and Mira.

"I really promise."

The silence in the apartment had been constant for a long time when Albert finally noticed. He reluctantly clicked *save* and rose from his desk, stretching his arms above and behind him. In the living room, a clown face glowed from the television screen. Wide, filling the glass, grinning. Albert had trouble looking too long at it, felt an itch on his fingers and neck. Nicky was gone, perhaps to bed after waiting too long for his father to change his mind. Albert reached down and turned off the television, looked at the clock. Almost two hours since Nicky had come in to beg that he join them.

With the screen dark, he wondered if that really had been a clown on the screen.

Mira was asleep on the couch. No, that wasn't right. She was bent backward, twisted in contorted pain. Streams of blood dried in tributaries from her nose and eyes, smeared in places where they had wiped against the off-white cushions.

"Mira?" He should have run to his wife, held her, called 911. But nothing felt real. The air was thick, an after-image of a massive explosion which he did not see nor smell. A quiet sense of abandonment.

He looked away from Mira—*just sleeping*—and walked across the room, down the hall towards Nicky's bedroom. He was calm, his pulse accelerating only when he opened the door and clicked the light to an empty room, sheets tightly tucked by Mira that morning. Albert checked the bathroom, his own room, the kitchen. His son was gone. Only when certain of this did he return to the living room, lay two fingers to his wife's throat as he'd seen them do on television, not certain what he was searching for. Finally, and for a long while, he screamed and wailed over his dead wife and missing son.

Everyone on their floor was dead. All had been watching television, either *The Show* or something else equally mundane. In the few apartments he'd checked, having to kick in the loosely-bolted doors after minutes of unanswered knocking, he saw the clown face on the television and looked away as soon as his fingers and neck began to itch. Once he tried changing the channel. In the corner of his eye he saw more faces on the screen, sometimes the same, sometimes narrower and dark.

Never once did he feel like a trespasser, though he did wonder if this was simply a dream and he was sleepwalking into his neighbors' homes. Two floors down Albert broke into the McGovern place and drifted slowly through their rooms. Two boys in elementary school, the youngest a year older than his own, and a daughter a freshman in high school. He found none of them. Only the unmoving, dry-blood adults on the couch.

No one answered 911 when, at last, he tried to call. Not knowing what to do, he went back to his own apartment and slept on the living room floor beside his dead wife. Part of him expected to wake from the dream any moment.

Two hours before sunrise, Mira rose up and tried to kill him. Closed her mouth around his bicep and tried to rip the skin free. Eyes bloody and unfocused, teeth closing tighter over her husband's arm, biting down hard and hard and hard—

*   *   *   *

Dinneck woke shouting and flailing against the pews. *Bang. Bang* against the wood, as if to dislodge the woman's mouth from his arm again. That first night Dinneck had been forced to slam Mira's head against the coffee table to make her let go. Seeing later how the New Race's teeth were so effectively pointed, sharpened either by their own hand or the same metamorphosis which made their skin hard and crusty, Dinneck knew he'd been lucky. Mira's teeth.... but he couldn't finish the thought. He'd gone too far just now in classifying his wife with no more concern that the millions of other Shufflers who came up from Below when the sun fell away.

The rhythmic pad-pad-pad of running outside, along the alley, flirting shapes barely visible past the stained glass windows. The sound followed the Passion of Christ, depicted in wood panels along the church walls, heading for the nave. The main church doors were closed, but never locked. No need. Not this soon.

The running steps scrabbled at the door, lingering longer than last night. Curled fist/claw on the wood. Bang. Bang. Bang. Running away in new pursuit, or simple fleeing the building's lingering power. Silence. Candles hissed across the church. They'd pounded on the door, he realized, not merely banged once for effect as they usually did.

The strength of the church was weakening quickly. Dinneck had felt, almost *tasted*, its power when he first arrived three days ago, It wasn't surprising that first night when the Shufflers dared not even the lowest steps leading from the street. Runners stayed their advances, never daring to run as close as they apparently had tonight.

Like the previous church, Saint Agnes, his refuge was weakening to the point Dinneck felt his security melt whisky-ice thin. Wedged between the Monroe Financial building and a nameless, behemoth brick office, Christ the King church would last him perhaps only this final night.

When God gathered everyone's children in his arms and left the world for the demons to run slipshod across the globe, the churches seemed to remain filled with the Lord's love and protection. Doors carefully closed to prevent spilling. Once Dinneck moved in, the seal was broken and God's power leaked slowly into the stale air outside, drained like a flashlight left on under a child's pillow.

He took up residence in Saint Agnes after fleeing his apartment, four weeks and an eternity ago. The *Holy Light* shone into the eyes of the New Race when they pursued, blinding them, keeping them at a respectful distance. It faded a little every day, until three nights ago when a Runner turned the knob and opened the door, exposing Saint Agnes to the cool night air. Dinneck saw only the arm, long and moorish brown in the afterglow of the wind-flickered candles. The Runner never entered, though for a moment Dinneck had felt a horrible thrill that he might at last see these creatures whose night-shrouded footsteps marked their presence, but of whom he'd seen only flashing glimpses through colored glass.

The Shufflers, however, had come in that night, uncertain and wary. Dinneck huddled on the altar, watching the candles sputter in death, hearing the slow, uncertain steps of the walking dead, the *stolen* dead, moving up the center aisle. He'd curled into a ball behind the altar, squeezing whatever remained of God's love from the narthex, sucking the last of the holiness from the air and praying it would last until daylight.

It had.

When he dared look up the next morning, a single sun-stricken body, its captive soul burned free in the light, lay crumpled in the aisle beside the front pew. The man's face peeled in thick lines at the cheeks, as if someone's fingers had once been drawn down into them. Probably so. A person could not fight these creatures once in their grip, except to flail uselessly at whatever dead flesh they could before being rent and torn into their own death.

Those were good deaths, however. The victim who made the marks on that dead thing's cheeks would not be coming back as a vessel for another demon. There would be nothing left.

Now, Dinneck looked about the dim interior of Christ the King. It was happening here, the fading of the protection, sooner than Dinneck would have thought. Cracks in the walls, maybe, windows never quite closed. Heaven's heat dissipating. He needed a new haven—church or synagogue or Hindu temple—once the sun returned. He'd had been lucky in Saint Agnes. Not again, not if he stayed here past morning.

How long before he ran out of sanctified ground and became trapped in the middle of Route One as daylight winked out and night fell on him like a net? If he made it out of downtown, maybe north into Somerville or Medford, he might find a haven for a night. Maybe bide his time until he reached the suburbs. How many churches were there in Burlington that hadn't already been sucked dry by some other desperate survivor?

Maybe the waterfront held the answer. Steal a boat, sail away. Until his food ran out, and he died slowly, to have his body raped by a grinning imp from Hell, riding back to shore to join the swarming hive of hard shell corpses in the darkness of the MBTA subway tunnels.

Dinneck picked up the notebook. His *New Race Dictum* had grown one page at a time, hurried scrawls of Bic pen on sweat-dropped paper. One of his earliest thoughts was that he'd been spared to chronicle these times. Later, to pay God for the continued stay of his execution, he preached in the deserted streets, trying to bring the people back with his words.

They weren't listening. God was gone. He and the children were on some far away planet, green grass, fields and clouds, Nicky and the McGovern boys laughing and running down hills, swimming in clear, clear lakes. Not for the first time Dinneck appreciated the irony of the true Rapture. All those well-dressed Jehovah's Witnesses, now walking slack among the neighborhoods, ripping warm flesh off shoulders and bellies. The Rapture came, but only the children could ride.

Dinneck drained the last of his canteen. The water was sour, had been when first poured from the plastic jug in the convenience store at the end of the block. Everything more sour each day, more meaningless. He rose from the bench and walked towards the main doors of the church. His steps were silenced by the carpet, but any Dead waiting outside the door would feel his heat, the ripples in the air of a living, beating heart. Blood not yet cold and sagging in unused veins.

The vessel containing the holy water was half full. He lifted the plastic bowl from its wall-mounted base and removed the square of sponge from the center. He squeezed what water he could back into the bowl and drank, stopping only at the sucking of his mouth on dry plastic. The water spread through him, clean, fresh and powerful. It reached his furthest corners, set his fingers and toes to curl involuntarily.

Dinneck felt alive in this brief moment, as if he was still a true child of God. Orphaned, yes, but still His Child. Perhaps Dinneck's body was now the sole vessel of this building's power. The thought set him on edge. He stared at the outer doors, waiting for them to burst open.

His body, his blood now the vessel.

Dinneck looked away from the doors, and understood.

His preaching was not in vain. It simply was not enough. The body and blood of redemption was needed. The realization frightened him. But since walking into the living room and finding his wife on the couch, his son gone, something evil and horrible on the television screen, this decision felt right. The missing ingredient in what remained of his Mission.

He would die, yes. But he would die *well*, unlike those who fell to the street clutching their heart, or stumbled from a ledge to the sidewalk three stories below. When Dinneck died, there would be nothing left of his body. Nothing left of his soul for the demons to infest and manipulate. He would become diluted, nonexistent, cleansing energy coursing through the guts of the Demon World below him. And perhaps, Dinneck might gather some souls for God along the way.

He returned to the bench and the open notebook. Why had he bothered? Soon there would be no one left to read the Dictum. Still, he sat and raised the pen. One final chapter to explain for anyone finding these words what they needed to do, to serve God, to be free at last.

* * * *

It took most of the next morning in Christ the King's sacristy to locate the reserves of holy water. He held the glass jar in his hand, feeling the weight of his mission. Did they bless the water only when they poured it into the receiving bowls? He broke the seal, unscrewed the cap. No smell, save the sensation of dampness around the lid. Glass to his lips.

He drank in heavy, wanting gulps. The Power was immense, heavy, *too much*, filling the bag of his stomach, reaching through his veins with the electric fingers of God Himself. He wanted to stop, wanted to drop the jar and spew the water. *This is wrong, I am wrong.* Still he drank, until he could hold no more.

The interior of the church was too bright, too much sun through the stained glass. He swallowed air, forcing the water down. Albert Dinneck was now the vessel, and must not break. He stumbled, rocking like a boat in a storm, down the aisle. Near the back of the church his Work lay discarded. He felt it crying out to him in a silent wail of abandonment.

Along the streets, feeling shards of sunlight cut through his skin, tunnel vision in his new state of Grace, to the entrance to the subway's Red Line. Concrete stairs fell into darkness. Down there lurked the monsters. Blood and other unknowable fluids stained the sidewalk, more so near the mouth of this New Hell. That was where he now traveled—Hell. Preach among its denizens a sermon of hope and redemption. Reach into their mouths and free the souls trapped within.

Down the steps, slowly, his stomach stretched painfully. He needed to pee, but knew he could not. *Must* not.

The smell of decomposition, garbage too long in the sun, scent of rotting banana peels and vinegar. At the bottom of the steps he stared into deep pockets of darkness broken only by secondary light streaming from the stairwell behind him, or through various ventilation slats overhead. Still, he saw well enough, the Light in him shining through his eyes into the murk. Maybe it was just his memory of the station's layout playing out in his mind, a mental map translated to vision.

The turnstile clicked as he passed through. Spackled blood dried below the red-painted stripe denoting the MBTA subway line. Both blood and stripe were dark gray shades in this lightless world. He stepped onto the platform. Empty. No lights, the twin open mouths of the tunnel on either side. He would stay here. They would come to him.

Dinneck considered preaching some more, as he used to do in the safety of the light above. His bladder ached. So much power running through him, he dared not break its spell.

Shuffling feet from the tunnel mouths, worn shoes on dust, dry feet whispering. Soon the shapes. Shufflers, too many to count, following his heat and blood scent, emerging from both sides. Dinneck moved to the center of the platform, heart racing. His instincts screamed for him to run back through the turnstiles and into the sun. One more day, one more week, the Power protecting him at night might last *that* long.

Perhaps this was how Jesus felt seeing the soldiers marching up the hill to arrest him. Dinneck could not leave. He must die today. He was now the two fish with which God would feed the masses. The two walls of lumbering bodies merged together, silent save their steps. They stopped. A sound like a police siren, organic and wet, sent them into uncertain hesitancy.

A Runner came up the abandoned tracks, so fast Dinneck thought for a moment it was a train. It scrabbled onto the platform. The Shufflers moved aside, a demonic Moses parting them like the sea. The creature reared up. Tall, with strong, muscular legs bent nearly ninety-degrees to prevent it from hitting the ceiling. Its segmented body glistened as if adorned with flakes of mica. Dinneck could not make out many details, but could see its *shape* clearly enough. Large growths, like many heads along the front and sides of its body, four arms, two where one would expect them, two more reaching from behind like the bones of old wings. The Runner's head sloped small and narrow, bird-like. The overall effect was utterly alien. Dinneck fought an instant revulsion—like looking too closely at the surreal features of a wasp, magnified a hundredfold. He wanted to run. *It* wanted him to run, if only to catch him again for sport.

The legs bent further, the body leaned forward, arms supporting the awkward bulk by slapping onto the concrete floor. He was being studied. The Shufflers, those for whom he'd come, moved closer. The Runner hissed/screamed its siren call. The others stopped, uncertain, wanting to devour the man standing before them but apparently not at the expense of this demon's ire.

Dinneck suddenly thought he understood the nature of these Runners. They were shepherds, former wolves who now, after stealing the sheep, protect their captives from their own ignorance and blind wanderings. *Dinneck* was now the wolf, and the beast before him stared through dull red-glowing slits, deciding if he was a threat.

"I am here to die," Dinneck whispered. His tongue stuck to the roof of his dry mouth. He forced himself to swallow, then added in a louder voice, "I am an offering from God who has left this world to your devices."

The Runner hissed. On either side, its flock moved forward and were allowed to pass. The Runner, slowly, moved back onto the tracks to wait, and watch.

A dozen arms grabbed Dinneck's shirt, pulled him forward. He closed his eyes. He tried not to think, tried to send himself back to his old apartment, when Mira and Nicky were alive. An overwhelming need to run and survive gripped him as tight as the dead, hard-crusted fingers. The mass of Shufflers poured over him like a wave, pressed him to the floor. No hot breath on his neck, only the icy feel of teeth pressing down, splitting his flesh, the warmth of his own blood. Fire, ice, screaming pain through his body. Clothes and skin were torn away. A chunk of his leg pulled free, the stale air racing across his exposed arteries and muscle burned like acid. *Was* acid. So many on him, he couldn't thrash or try to fight.

Dinneck was turned onto his back. Eyes still closed he managed one final scream before a mouth bit down on his chin, throat. Fingers peeled back his cheeks and eyelids, but he saw nothing.

*   *   *   *

The Runner on the tracks watched the feeding with relieved contentment. There were more Shufflers far back in the tunnels, pushing forward, pressing against those in front of them in their need to consume, to taste even a drop of this new blood. The heat of the victim bathed the platform with an intoxicating glow in their eyes.

Something changed. Where once a pulsing mound of Shuffler bodies heaved and writhed atop Dinneck's body, the Runner now noticed many of its kin no longer moved. Others, impatient, shoved them aside, scrounged with dry lips what might be left, shards of bones, bloody rivulets squeezed away from the feeding.

The mound of bodies grew.

The demon on the tracks noticed too late what was happening. It howled and leapt onto the platform, shoving its way through, tossing Shufflers, both moving and still, aside.

There was little left of Dinneck's body. Wads of flesh, fluid spilled across the floor only to be covered by a desperate black tongue. A long white bone protruding from the mouth of another, though the mouth no longer moved. The Runner swatted at a piece of intestine and felt its preternatural flesh burn. It backed away, screamed again. Still the horde pressed past it, not just in hunger, now driven by something awakening inside them, desperate for the communion being offered.

Eventually there was nothing left of the man but multi-hued stains on the concrete, heavy lumps of Dinneck's flesh buried within the unmoving Shuffler bodies. When the smell and heat dissipated the mob moved back into the tunnel, leaving the Runner to shove the empty husks of its lost flock off the platform and onto the tracks. It didn't know what else to do for the moment. Its hand still burned where it had touched the victim's flesh.

*   *   *   *

Dinneck moved through the clouds into the vastness of space. He sensed others with him but could not look to see who they were. He waited for the Light of God to appear from the star-filled dark and embrace him.

Further, further into the cold of the universe he traveled, always waiting for the ethereal doors of heaven to open and swallow him into the Light. Somewhere there was the green grass and fields where his son played. He wanted to believe Mira was one of the freed souls traveling with him. Had she been there, in the subway? Maybe. He had to believe, have faith.

They traveled out, out, into the black void, calling with silent voices. Waiting for the embrace. Waiting for the answer.

About "Tanner's Bomb"

Wow, you're still with me? That's great. We save one of my favorites for last. Personally, I think this is one of funniest stories I've written. Only one other person that I know of thinks that, too. Everyone else has commented that it's one of my scariest pieces. Trust me, it's not. It's funny. And scary. Funny and scary.

Anyway, "Tanner's Bomb" isn't the original name. When I first concocted the idea for this story, my wife Janet and I were on a five hour bus trip to New York City with Kevin and Connie McCarthy. Our own bus was overbooked, so they put us in with a church group from town, and we had to sit separately. I guess even the ecclesiastical nature of the passengers had no sway in letting me sit with my wife—still, they had Bingo, so that was something.

With nothing to keep me company but my own imagination and an older woman who slept for most of the ride, I decided to come up with a bizarre title and see if I could conjure a story to go with it. At that moment a Christmas tree truck drove by (those flatbed tractor-trailers rigged up every holiday season to carry trees to various gas stations and mall parking lots). So, I had the first part of the title: "As the Christmas Tree Truck Drives By…" but I needed something to go with it. Since I was in a sour mood, I decided on "Spit".

Over the next five hours, between spurts of Bingo, I wrote in my head the story "As the Christmas Tree Truck Drives By, Spit." Of course, before I decided to market it, I changed the name to the much simpler: "Tanner's Bomb". It has since become, in my mind, a must-read classic for every holiday season.

Tanner's Bomb

"I'm so sorry. I just wanted to help. So many dead...."

"It's OK. Have some more apple cider. Relax." Detective McGovern guided the arm holding the styrofoam cup up until the man took a drink of his own accord. Max Tanner winced, then took another sip. The smell of smoke drifting off his leather jacket overpowered the spicy tang in the air of the greenhouse. He looked at the detective.

"Did you go see? Did someone go see?"

"Yes. Some of the residents were sent to Pelham Medical Center for treatment. Some sort of a catatonic shock. We'll see what the doctors have to say. DSS is sending a crew to look after all the children. But no bodies. Mister Tanner, did you hear me? They found no bodies."

Max stared into the steam rising from his cup. "No bodies." He took a sip. "No, I suppose there wouldn't be."

A uniformed officer with a day's stubble staining his face said, "All right, that's enough. Let's just take this guy to—"

The detective raised his hand. "Maybe you should tell us exactly what happened, Mister Tanner. From the beginning." He looked at his watch. "Just keep to the highlights. It IS Christmas Eve...."

Max thought about that. Christmas Eve. Had someone told Pam and the boys? Daddy wouldn't be coming home. Daddy was a murderer. An overwhelming sadness gripped him, both for himself and the people of that damned town. He looked at the large Christmas tree standing unlit by the door.

"Promise you'll leave that tree unplugged?"

The detective nodded. "Yes, we promise. Tell us what happened."

Max told them. "It started when I had to go to the bathroom…"

*   *   *   *

Max joined Bing Crosby in an off-key rendition of "Chestnuts Roasting…" as the eighteen wheeler lumbered along the two-lane highway. Massive pines stood along both sides of the road, in silent respect to their fallen comrades. Laying in state on the flat-bed, one hundred and fifty scotch pine and spruce crowded between makeshift railings. Soon to be Christmas trees, on their way to Pelham and a hundred and fifty cozy homes. One of them belonged to the Tanner family. As a weak but acceptable incentive for this last-minute delivery, Max had his choice of the best tree of the run. All he had to do was drop off the one hundred forty-nine others at Henson's "Tree Farm," then ten minutes later he'd be home. Not a bad deal all around. From under the passenger seat poked the oversized Wal-Mart bag with three sets of tree lights.

Max sang and glanced at the map. He should have hit Holy Refuge by now. The red circle surrounding the village's borders made it easy to spot. As did the words "Stay Away!" with an arrow pointing to said circle. Normally Max followed Bart's scattered map notes, but not tonight. He was fifteen minutes ahead of schedule and really had to find a bathroom. The town, seemingly dropped in the middle of the northern Massachusetts Berkshires, was the only option aside from ruining his pants or squatting in the woods somewhere. The latter was never an option in his mind.

A robed figure suddenly appeared over the rise, leaning awkwardly on a walking stick. Max downshifted and rolled down the window.

Frigid air blasted into the cab. He never got a chance to ask for directions. As the truck rolled within yelling distance, the white-haired man raised both the gnarled walking stick and the hood of his robe over his head. He signed himself clumsily and disappeared into the late-afternoon shadows of the forest.

The truck drifted by the spot where Max *thought* he'd seen a man having a seizure. Nobody there.

"Loony bastard." He shut off the radio. A group of teenage boys ran into the woods just ahead of him. Long hoods flew from their heads as they faded into the trees.

Great, Max thought. *I'm driving into a cult.* The headlights limited his vision in the increasing gloom. He downshifted again, looked for an entrance to somewhere, anywhere.

There it was. A dirt road; too small for the rig, but it'd be worth a look-see. The gears hissed and barked. The truck rolled to a stop at the path's entrance.

"Holy Refuge, I presume," Max whispered. Houses at the top of the hill huddled close, clustered in deepening circles around a dimly lighted common. He couldn't see much more from this vantage point. A crowd of monk-like townspeople, ropes dangling at their waists, ran toward him.

Max rolled up his window.

As they approached, the group slowed. Hoods concealed most of their faces. One figure moved cautiously forward. Various unrecognizable gestures accompanied each step. Max began to wonder if this was a deaf-person cult. He pressed the emergency break and opened the door. A little.

"You can't stop here," the man within the robe said. He was clearly distressed, diverting his eyes from the cab. Max felt braver. He opened the door the rest of the way and stepped down. He bent to look into the cowl.

"Hi, there. My name's Max Tanner. Didn't mean to scare you."

The man didn't look at him. "Hello, Max. I'm David. Please, I saw the sign on your door. You drive for Callebri Brothers?"

"Yea, that's right. Listen, all I need is to use—"

"We have an agreement with the owner. Bartholomew Callebri. You aren't suppose to be here."

"Oh, really," Max said, then remembered the red circle. "Well, no, I guess I'm not." The cramps sent him a painful reminder. "Listen. Do you have a bathroom?" Four robed men emerged from the woods next to the trailer. They hunkered down on the roadside; began drawing pictures in the dirt. One of them lowered his hood. Gray hair stuck out like a clown's wig. He was old, wrung-out and twisted like the walking staffs they carried. The clown-haired man, eyes closed, raised his face to the truck. He opened two fingers scissor-like to his lips, then hacked a wad of spit towards the trailer. It landed on a wooden rail, dripped onto a pine branch.

"What the hell…?" The crowd gasped. Hands emerged from drooping sleeves, pressed against unseen ears. The man called David took a half step forward, eyes still cast down.

"Please, sir. Max, is it? You shouldn't use such language."

"That…old person just spit on my truck." As he spoke, he saw in his peripheral vision another of the four rise and begin a rapid series of bat-bat-bats with his staff against one of the tires.

David spoke quickly. "Please, Max. Please understand. We mean neither you, nor your vehicle, any harm. We're a peaceful people. It's just that—"

Max was not there. He stood in front of the old man, wrenching away the staff and tossing it into the woods. The monk turned and ran after it. By the time David reached him, Max was kicking at the drawings along the road.

"They promised us no one would come. We send them money every month. They promised us you would not carry…those…." he gestured towards the horizontal trees "…things near our town."

Max paced back and forth. "They're just Christmas trees!"

Gasps and shrieks and covered ear locations. Max turned to the crowd and shouted, "What's your problem? Christmas Trees!" Shrieks and gasps. "Christmas Trees!" This was getting fun.

David grabbed his arm with surprising force. "Please, we strive to be a spiritual people. We recognize the holiness in everything around us. The sky, snow, and most especially the trees are precious gifts from God." The grip seemed to tighten for a moment on Max's arm. "What you are delivering to so many unfortunate souls is an abomination to all that we have been taught to be sacred. These fallen symbols of heaven will become the idols of Satan, representing with brilliant and horrifying clarity the path the world has taken."

His hand dropped, as if the words fell too heavily upon him to keep the grip on the driver. He continued, "Evil has triumphed over the world, is slowly working its way towards our town, our homes…" His face, one of painful sadness. "…our last refuge in God's embrace."

Max swallowed. He looked at the tired man in front of him. David was probably younger than him but showed lines of fatigue Max wouldn't likely see in himself until middle age. He looked back at the truck, idling patiently behind him. Then, slowly, he smiled.

"But, these are just Christmas trees."

Shrieks and wails. David's face reddened within his cowl. "Get out of here, sir. Now. We have a deal with your superiors. God forgive my impatience, but you simply do not understand."

Max turned and hopped into the cab. He grabbed the keys and killed the engine. The background rumble of the diesel cut out. The group stood in stunned silence.

"Listen," he said, jumping back down. "If you think…stop hitting my truck!" The monk had re-emerged from the woods and resumed his punishment against a tire. Beside him, one of the kneelers spat on the trailer.

"That's it!" Max said. "I'm going to the bathroom. Your bathroom! When I come back, if any part of my rig is damaged, you'll meet my 'superiors' face-to-face. Or at least their lawyers." More shrieks.

"You cannot—"

"I can. The sooner you show me to the potty the sooner I'll leave." Max pushed past him. The crowd shuffled aside like a human Red Sea. Max sensed the anger of the leader behind him, but he was gambling violence wasn't in the rule books. Halfway up the dirt path, he heard David shout, "Nathan! Show that man where to go then bring him directly back here. Do not speak to him. Quickly now."

By the time Max reached the common he'd been joined by a teenage boy, dressed in his own dark robes. Neither spoke.

The common glowed with lanterns. Small yellow flames danced in glass cages. Similar light drifted from the clusters of single-story houses. No electricity, Max mused.

Like the ghost of Christmas Future, the boy pointed to a narrow structure on the far side of the common. An outhouse, no doubt.

* * * *

The detective raised his hands. "Listen," he said. "This is all well and fine, but until the doctors tell us what happened to those people I don't see how—"

"There were others," Max whispered, still looking into his cup of cider.

McGovern looked at his watch then leaned forward in the chair. "If there are others, then why can't we find them? You brought us in here saying people were dead. Unless you're able to tell us how that happened, I think we should call it a night. We'd like to be with our families."

Max shuddered involuntarily. "If you'll just let me finish."

A chilly gust of wind swept through the room. A women in a skirted business suit, a badge dangling from her waist, closed the door and glanced icily at Max. She covered her mouth to whisper into the detective's ear. Slowly, McGovern's face went pale, then hardened. When the woman finished she straightened, obviously waiting for direction. McGovern looked up at her and said softly, "They were burned?"

The styrofoam cup disappeared within Max's hands. Cool cider poured over his fingers. The woman looked at the truck diver with obvious contempt.

"Yes, sir," she said. "At least a half-dozen they're guessing. The bone fragments were sent to Amherst for analysis."

The detective said nothing for a minute. He simply stared between his legs at the floor. When he looked up, Max knew things would get nasty very quickly. "Mister Tanner, I mentioned when we first arrived that you should call a lawyer. I strongly recommend that now. The charges against you have been upgraded to suspicion of murder. Do you understand me? Mister Tanner?"

"I didn't mean to hurt anyone. How could I know?"

McGovern looked behind the prisoner. "John, did you read him his rights?" John nodded. "Mister Tanner, would you like to have officer Jamison repeat your rights? Let me remind you that everything you say is being considered a confession."

Max waved away the warning. "I understand my rights. I didn't know people would die."

The detective stared at him in silence for a moment, then checked the tape recorder. "Finish your story, please. If at any time you wish to discontinue this confession and contact a lawyer please understand you may do so."

"Yes. Yes, I know." Suddenly Max realized he would never be with Pam again. Never play baseball with the boys. He began to cry. The others in the room stared dispassionately at him, waiting for the story to resume.

*   *   *   *

If anything was evil in the world, Max decided, it would be outhouses. Once outside, fresh clean air swept over him like a lover. His spirits were decidedly up. The silent teenager stood a few paces away, glancing nervously across the common. Max followed his gaze. From their vantage, the truck and townsfolk were out of sight.

"Nathan, is it?"

The boy nodded.

"I'm sorry. What did you say?"

"Yes," Nathan said.

"It's OK. I won't tell them you talked to me." The boy tried in vain to suppress a smile. Max pressed the advantage. "That guy. David. He's the boss?"

"Well, I guess. He's my Dad. People rely on him a lot when the world gets too close."

"Too close. Hmm." They were all nuts. Max was officially five minutes behind schedule now. It was Christmas Eve, and these people were hiding in their hoods like kids in a thunderstorm. This time of year, bringing Christmas to New England from the cab of his truck, Max almost felt like Santa Claus...though he decided not to share that image with young Nathan.

"Do you believe all that stuff your Dad was saying, about Christmas trees?" Max noticed the boy didn't shriek at the words. In fact, he didn't even wince.

"My father believes it." He kicked at a rock that was frozen into the ground. "Maybe not as much as Grandfather, but the elders are a very spiritual people." Max wanted to interrupt and ask why religious fanatics insisted on calling old people "elders," but held his tongue.

"Grandfather...." Nathan continued. "He believes in the teachings. In fact, he was the primary drafter of the new edition of the *Book of God's Laws*." He looked up, an almost-smile forming under the cowl. When Max didn't offer the expression of awe the boy apparently expected, he looked back at the tops of his shoes. "I don't know. I suppose you get out of your faith what you want to. The elders are very wise. They wouldn't believe in all of this if it wasn't true." The implied "would they?" hung in the air between them.

"Well," Max said, trying not to sound overly condescending. "I'm sure it's true to them." As he spoke, his gaze fell on a twisted Maple, standing alone in the center of the common. An uncomfortable idea began to glow in his head. "What about you?" he said. "The other kids your age?"

Nathan shrugged his shoulders, began to say something then stopped. He raised his head, letting his gaze linger on the path leading back towards the road. He said, "We have to get back now. You shouldn't be here."

The idea was a forest fire in Max's mind. *Oh hell*, he thought. *Maybe it'll be fun.* The only question was how to get some juice. The idea brightened further. *If you need power, get a battery.*

"Listen, Nathan. Do you people have a car? You know, drive?" He made a steering gesture with his hands.

"I know what a car is, sir. We may be religious, but we're not stupid."

"Right. Sorry. Then there's a car around here?"

"We have an old Chevy out back. Once a month someone gets special dispensation to go to Pelham for supplies. It's never a happy time. But they won't let children go." He paused. "Why?"

"I was just thinking. It's so nice here, I might just stay for a day or two."

Nathan stepped back, then turned away. He looked as if he were deciding whether to run screaming for help. Still looking across the common, he said, "You can't stay here. They won't let you. Please, you've caused enough trouble. Leave us alone."

Max smiled. "Tell you what. We'll make a deal. You give me something, a gift maybe, and I'll leave. I'll even make it look like you forced me out."

Nathan looked back at him. "What kind of gift?"

"Go get the battery out of that car and bring it here. That's it. My Chrysler at home is dead. You give me your battery to take home with me, and I'll be gone faster than your townspeople can scream."

"That's stealing."

"Not if you give it to me. That's my offer."

After a moment's thought, "I'm not supposed to leave you."

"Take it or leave it."

He watched the boy running toward a dilapidated shed across the grounds. Max wasn't sure if his plan could technically work, but it'd be worth seeing their expressions when he tried.

Once Nathan disappeared from sight, so did Max. He emerged from the trees onto the narrow stretch of highway, a hundred yards up-road from the truck. It still suffered under the spitting and battering of the old men. David was there, glancing nervously up the path. Max would have to do this quickly. Under the cover of the darkness, he ran across the road into the trees beyond.

* * * *

Everyone wore black shoes. They poked in and out of the robes on the other side of the trailer. The old men knelt along the roadside. Max stepped slowly, quietly. Flickering light from lanterns cast wavering shadows around the rig. One foot on the cab's step. His eyes rose above the passenger window. There was David, looking the other way. Max's heart beat out the excitement and fear of the moment. He'd come this far.

Be quick. The lock was up. This was a good thing, since keys make noise. He lifted the door handle.

Click. The inner dome light snapped on. Max whispered, "Shit."

Voices. He reached under the seat and grabbed the Wal-Mart bag. It crinkled its plastic scream as he jumped down.

"Who's there?" David's voice. Footsteps. Max ran into the woods. As he moved between the trees he took hold of the tangled mass of Christmas lights and tossed the white bag away. No sense giving them a beacon. He ran parallel with the road. A quick look behind revealed dark figures moving into the woods. They quickly changed direction and returned to the roadside.

"Mister Tanner!" David's voice again, more distant. At least they weren't following. Max had a good idea where they'd go next. Time was not on the side of this plan. He turned towards the road. Without checking if anyone was looking he crossed the pavement in four steps.

The common looked no different than when he left it, with the exception of a teenage boy standing near the outhouse, battery in his hand. Max ran to him. How long did he have? Sixty seconds? He giggled involuntarily.

Nathan sagged in relief when he saw Max approach, then abruptly stiffened when he noticed what hung from the man's fist. Though he'd never seen Christmas lights, he had a good idea that's what they were.

"Where did you go? What are those?"

"Never mind. Is that battery working?"

Nathan began to hand it over, then everything made sense. "Dear God! Those ARE lights! What are you doing?"

Max grabbed the battery with both hands, careful not to crush any of the small colored bulbs in the process. He ran to the maple in the center of the common. Distant voices drifted up from the roadside, growing louder.

Max took out a pocket knife from his coat, cut the ties binding the wires. It took an eternity to sort through the chaotic mess and hook the three sets together. A yellow glow spilled onto the grass from the pathway.

Here they come. He cut the plug from one free end, peeled apart the wires. He suddenly had to go to the bathroom again. He could barely make out the thin white line on the positive feed. "Good enough," he said aloud, then tossed the string of lights into the bare branches of the tree.

It caught in two places. The rest fell to the other side. Before Max could round the tree Nathan rammed into him like a linebacker. They rolled across the lawn.

"This is wrong," the boy puffed. "I have to stop you. You shouldn't be here." He was strong, but Max guessed Nathan was too afraid to realize it. He stood up, shoved the boy to the ground.

"You should thank me, kid. Christmas is for everybody. Even loonies." He tossed the wires back into the tree. Loops of lights hung like snakes.

"Mister Tanner!" The voice of Nathan's father. Max turned around. David power-walked across the common. Behind him, the townspeople followed with lanterns. A few others brandished burning torches. This wasn't good. The mob looked like something out of a Frankenstein movie. Behind the torch bearers, mothers tried in vain to usher children into their homes.

Out of time. Max ran to the other side of the tree. He re-emerged with the exposed wires and the battery. Nathan remained on the ground, uncertain of what to do. The horde was less than ten feet away. David suddenly stopped. His people did likewise. They stared first in wonder, then slowly-emerging horror at the tangle of wires draped across the maple. The elders of the group, both men AND women this time, pushed their way through the crowd and kneeled without fear before Max and his demon. Sticks pounded the ground. Spit poured like wine towards the tree roots.

David said, "What...what are those?" His voice was shaky, like a child seeing something he didn't understand, but was pretty sure he didn't like it.

Max knelt and pulled apart the wire ends. Positive in his left, negative in his right. He hoped. Even if this didn't work (and he was more and more certain it wouldn't as the seconds ticked by), it was all worth seeing the wonder-struck expression of the crowd.

"What, THESE?" he said. "Let's just say it's an early Christmas present." David's glaring expression left no room for doubting it was now or never. Max shrugged and smiled. "Ho. Ho. Ho!"

He lowered the wires to the battery.

Color and light exploded from the tree. Reds, greens, yellows, blues, falling across the faces of the townsfolk. The elders lifted wrinkled hands in defense. As one, they opened their mouths to scream but made no sound. Faces twisted, elongating within frayed cowls. Their skin stretched and faded to burnt charcoal gray. Lights danced like swarms of flies about them. Then no features at all, just light. The robes fell to the ground, covering piles of ash.

Like a vampire facing the rising sun, David's face hollowed and sunk, retreating from the colors dancing across it. Behind him, others stood likewise, in painful rapture of the splendor.

The battery glowed brighter and brighter. As in a nightmare, Max couldn't move, couldn't cry out. His hands were held by a preternatural gravity. A burning shape writhed within the battery, two red eyes opening in the midst of the Die Hard.

"Stop it! Stop it!" Nathan dove across the abyss into Max's face. The connection broke. As he rolled and pushed the boy off of his chest, Max saw the Christmas lights explode in a hundred tiny pops. He clambered to his knees to look back at the motionless crowd.

One by one, the residents of Holy Refuge sagged to their knees as if in prostration. They fell forward, faces hitting the ground in a group thud.

Everything became very quiet.

Then figures stirred, moving slowly at first. The children walked, then ran to their parents, screaming at them to wake up. Nathan moved to his father's prone body, turned him over, cradled the pale expressionless face in his lap.

"Dad? Father? Wake up! Please?" He looked at one of the discarded robes in front of him. "Grandfather?"

This was too much. Max walked to the boy's side.

"Is…is he all right?" The question woke not only Nathan but the rest of the children from their terror. Anger and hatred, all turned toward the stranger, activating alarm bells in every part of Max's body.

Fight or Flight. Better Run Now.

"You ba…ba…bad person!" Nathan dropped his father's head like a bug-infested melon, stood and pointed. "He did it! He killed our families!"

Better Run Now. Better Run Now.

Max ran.

As one child then another moved to intercept, Max battered them aside. A forest of arms and fists. On the path leading away from the common, he looked back. The comparison to Frankenstein couldn't have been more appropriate. Nathan led the mob, a burning torch held in front of him. Others grabbed the remaining lights and were one step behind.

Max ran a bit faster.

One old man remained beside the truck, rapping his heavy staff rhythmically against the trailer bed. Max ignored him.

Keys. Where are the keys? Here. Which one? He jumped onto the step, opened the door and slammed it shut. *Which one? Here.* The torches and lanterns slid down the pathway like lava. *Key in the ignition. Half turn.* The glow plug activated. The red "Warming" light flashed. Max sat alone in the cab, waiting. "Come on…." His jaw ached from tension. The driver's window shattered, a torn arm grabbed his throat.

Nathan screamed, "I'll kill you, you son of a…I'll kill you!" The boy meant what he almost said. Max gripped his own shaking fingers in a fist and pistoned them into Nathan's face. The boy fell away.

The green "Ready" light flashed. *Press the clutch. Turn the key.* The engine roared to life. In the side mirror, Max watched the mob toss their lanterns and torches over the railings, into the pile of hapless trees.

Max released the clutch. *Shift. Gas. Shift.* He drove as fast as possible without risking stalling the engine.

Bright, fiery sparks shot into the air. The last of the children fell from the burning truck, while others searched for rocks to throw after it. The eighteen-wheeler raced around a corner like a comet, then was gone.

* * * *

Max stopped talking. He still held the broken cup.

McGovern, realizing the story was over, leaned back in the metal folding chair.

"Mister Tanner," he said finally. "That was quite a thrilling tale. Though none of us want in any way to affect your testimony, are you sure that's what you want to say?"

Max shook his head. "I swear to God, it's all true. My truck. You saw my truck! Ruined. Burned away." His voice faded on the last words.

The stubble-faced officer behind Max stepped forward. "Sir, permission to continue this discussion another time? It's almost midnight, for God's sake. Bernie and I'll lock him up for the holidays. Maybe after he'll decide to tell us what really happened." As Jamison spoke, he moved towards the door.

Max thought of his words. Christmas was lost to him forever. Burned away in the faces of those pathetic old men and woman. He killed them. Then he noticed Jamison reaching behind the darkened Christmas tree.

"I think we can plug this thing back in, don't you?"

Max tried to stand. "No! Please don't—"

McGovern raised a hand in weak defiance. "John, now, leave it unplugged. We don't know—" But it was too late. The officer had the wires in the outlet.

Red and yellow lights stabbed like needles across the room, knocking Max back into his seat. They filled the driver's mouth and eyes. For a moment, he seemed to breath them in.

Then Max screamed.

Outside, "Chestnuts Roasting on an Open Fire" drifted like snow from the speakers, across the parking lot and the smoldering eighteen-wheeler. Christmas was in the air.

About the Author

Daniel G. Keohane is a novelist living, with his wife and three children, in the woods of New England among the salamanders and questionable raccoons. His horror stories have been published in various magazines and anthologies over the years. He is currently at work on his latest novel, and is an active member of the Horror Writers Association. For more information visit his website at **www.dankeohane.com**.

All author royalties for this book will be donated to the Central New England Multiple Sclerosis Society. For more information visit their website at **www.msnewengland.org**.

0-595-25664-3